At a time when families gather together in a spirit of joy and giving to celebrate our most beloved holiday, we are delighted to send this book to you.

Christmas seems the perfect time to express our thanks for your support and encouragement.

May the spirit of the season abide with you throughout the year and bring you peace and happiness.

Sincerely,
Harlequin Reader Service,
Christmas 1976

OTHER

Harlequin Romances

by VIOLET WINSPEAR

921—DESERT DOCTOR
1032—BELOVED TYRANT
1111—THE TOWER OF THE CAPTIVE
1318—PALACE OF THE PEACOCKS
1344—THE DANGEROUS DELIGHT
1434—THE CAZALET BRIDE
1472—BELOVED CASTAWAY
1514—THE CASTLE OF THE SEVEN LILACS
1555—RAINTREE VALLEY
1580—BLACK DOUGLAS
1616—THE PAGAN ISLAND
1637—THE SILVER SLAVE
1658—DEAR PURITAN
1680—RAPTURE OF THE DESERT

Many of these titles are available at your local bookseller
or through the Harlequin Reader Service.

For a free catalogue listing all available Harlequin Romances,
send your name and address to:

HARLEQUIN READER SERVICE,
M.P.O. Box 707, Niagara Falls, N.Y. 14302
Canadian address: Stratford, Ontario, Canada N5A 6W4

or use order coupon at back of books.

Blue Jasmine

by

VIOLET WINSPEAR

Harlequin Books

TORONTO • LONDON • NEW YORK • AMSTERDAM • SYDNEY • WINNIPEG

Original hardcover edition published in 1969
by Mills & Boon Limited

ISBN 0-373-01399-X

Harlequin edition published May 1970

Second printing May 1971
Third printing December 1976

Printed in Canada

CHAPTER ONE

THERE was a pensive air about the girl as she stood on the terrace of the hotel and gazed at the stars through the plumy crests of tall palm trees. She wore a blue silk evening dress, but she seemed withdrawn from the drifting dance music as she breathed the night air, redolent of jasmine and something wild and tangy that stole over the walls of the garden from the desert beyond.

This was the mysterious East her father had known and talked about; the land they had hoped to visit together. Beyond those walls lay the golden sands of her dreams, and early tomorrow she would ride alone to the Oasis of Fadna, where her father had lived in a desert house and painted the dawn and sunset pictures that had made his name as an artist. Such alive and vibrant pictures, awakening in the convent schoolgirl she had been at the time a longing to see the reality.

"We'll go, Lorna," her father had promised. "As soon as I'm well enough to travel, we'll go and live on the edge of the desert."

A germ from his travels had entered his system and Lorna had nursed him devotedly for a whole year in Paris. But slowly Peter Morel had succumbed to the fever and left his daughter alone

in the world. It was true she was not penniless—
Morel's artistry had made sure of that—but
nothing could make up for the loss of her lean and
quizzical father.

Even at this moment she could see him, smiling
lazily as he worked at his easel, or sketched an
unusual face with rapid strokes of the charcoal.

Her throat tightened, and her privacy at the far
end of the terrace felt invaded as footsteps
approached. They were masculine and she felt an
impatient urge to dart down the nearby steps and
lose herself in the garden. Even as she moved from
the shadows, the young man reached her side.

"There you are!" He gave an exasperated laugh.
"You promised me a dance, Lorna."

The music stole out from the lighted french
doors of the ballroom. The heat, the smoke from
cigaret, and the rather empty chatter had driven
her out into the night, and she wondered why
Rodney Grant should seek her out when there were
other girls who were frankly eager for his atten-
tions.

"Dancing bores me." The look she gave him
was cool. "I much prefer the fresh air and the way
those stars seem almost within reach of my hand."

"They are not, Lorna." His prosaic way of
speaking and looking at life always irritated her.
"Far better to accept what is within your reach."

"All the ordinary things?" she scoffed.
"Marriage and the chores that go with it, and being
taken for granted after a few years?"

"No man in his right senses could ever take you
for granted," he rejoined, and she heard that
slightly gruff note in his voice which meant he was

blushing. It amazed her that a grown man should stammer and blush because a girl happened to be presentable.

Lorna had silvery-gold hair, deep blue eyes, and a slender heart of a face, but she had been taught at her convent school that physical attributes were irrelevant and now she was out in the world she was hardly aware that men found her attractive. She was grateful for her good health, and the fact that she could ride a horse without tumbling off.

Suddenly there stole through the garden the plaintive sound of a reed flute, haunting and somehow beckoning in contrast to the dance music that had ceased for a while.

"Who plays that, I wonder?" Lorna moved nearer to the terrace wall and listened with an entranced light in her eyes. "I've heard it each night I have been here at the Ras Jusuf."

"It's probably one of the gardeners." Rodney came to her side, but when she felt the brush of his arm she drew away and ran down the terrace steps.

"Let's go and find this Arabian Pan who plays so alluringly among the trees," she said.

"You odd girl!" But Rodney followed where she led and soon they were deep in the garden among the towering palms and jacarandas with their drooping sprays of blossom.

"Oh," Lorna caught at a spray and gently crushed it, "can you breathe such air and not feel adventurous?"

"What do you mean by adventure?" Rodney teased. "Being alone with you like this makes me feel romantic."

"I'm not the romantic type," she rejoined.

"Well, not in the sense you mean. Life should hold some wonder, some quality of magic beyond empty kisses and empty promises."

"Have you never flirted with a man?" He stood in her path. "It can be fun to flirt, Lorna, and I should enjoy very much being your teacher."

"You wouldn't find me a very eager pupil, Mr. Grant." Her cool young voice had ice in it. "Unlike some of the other female visitors to the hotel I am not here to try and catch a husband."

"Don't tell me you came to see the desert?"

"Don't you consider the desert an intriguing place?" She turned away from him and listened to the hidden melody of the reed flute. It held all her attention. The chatter of Rodney Grant was an intrusion, but she was too polite to ask to be left alone.

"They'll be playing the last dance in the ballroom before long and you'll have missed it," she said hopefully.

"I couldn't leave you alone—with an Arab playing a flute somewhere among these trees."

"I'm not in the least nervous." She gave a laugh. "Tomorrow I shall be alone in the desert—"

"You can't seriously mean that?" He caught at her hand, but in a second she pulled free of his touch and drew away from him as if she couldn't tolerate physical contact with a man. The only male person she had even been close to had been her father, and only in the last year of his life had that been possible because before that he was always away on his travels, in search of unusual places to put on canvas.

Lorna's mother had died so long ago that she

could barely remember her, and much of her youth had been spent at convent school.

"When you are grown up," her father had said, "we'll travel the world together."

It was a dream to which she had clung all through their years apart, but it had not been meant to come true. Now at the age of twenty she came alone to the East, and alone she would go to the Oasis of Fadna, a sort of pilgrimage to the place her father had loved, and where he had made his home for several years.

"Now I've managed to get a good horse," she told Rodney, "I certainly intend to see something of the desert."

"You must let me come with you," he said firmly. "A girl like you can't go riding alone—why, parts of the desert are still untamed and lawless, and girls have been carried off and never been heard of again!"

Her laughter rang out, a faintly scornful note in it. "I am not Dolly Featherton," she scoffed. "You can't alarm me with tales of ardent and dangerous Arabs who carry off lonely girls to their *harems.* My father lived in the desert and he knew the *bedouin.* They prefer their own kind of woman and consider European females a little too bony."

"You are just being obstinate," Rodney said stiffly. "You could be kidnapped for ransom — oh, I'm glad you find that equally amusing! *Bedouins* assume that tourists are rolling in cash!"

"Then they'll be disappointed if they abduct me." She smiled and brushed a moth from her hair. "I have a reasonable income from the sale of some of my father's paintings, but I'm not rich—" And there she broke off as the haunting sound of the Arabian flute stole nearer. She listened and then darted beneath the arching fronds of the trees. She saw the glimmer of a pond on which water lilies floated, and there beside it crouched the figure of an Arab.

The hood of his *burnous* was pulled forward over his eyes, but Lorna saw the flute jutting from his lips. The melody petered out as he stared at her . . . in his monkish hood he was rather sinister.

Lorna's fingers clenched on her evening purse. She expected the usual request for *baksheesh,* but instead he put away the flute in the folds of his robes and gave her a dignified *salaam*.

"The *lella* seeks me out to have her fortune divined in the sand?" He spoke in French, which she spoke fluently herself, and his eyes gleamed in the shadow of his hood. "I have seem the *lella* in the bazaar, and I have seen her wandering in this garden. I think she is seeking something in the Land of the Veil."

Lorna gazed fascinated at the Arab, and then Rodney spoke scornfully at her shoulder. "Sand-divining? It's a lot of tomfoolery, Lorna. Don't waste your money on the old charlatan!"

"The *roumi* fears that he will have no place in the *lella's* destiny." With great composure the Arab drew a small bag from one of his capacious pockets. He pulled the drawstring and a stream of fine sand poured out on the path beside the pond. Lorna watched as he spread the pale sand with a dark hand and traced designs in it with his forefinger.

"I wish the *lella* to blow upon the sand, but lightly," he said.

She was about to kneel down on the ground when the diviner, with the instinctive gallantry of desert people, drew a scarf from about his neck and spread it upon the ground for her to kneel upon.

"*Merci,*" she smiled, and ignoring Rodney and his fumings she blew upon the strange designs in the sand. Then with bated breath she watched as the Arab studied the pattern into which the grains had settled.

"*Mektub,*" he murmured. "I see written here a house set in a lonely place, where the sands of the desert have encroached and smothered the flowers upon its walls. The *lella* should not go to this place, but it is written that she will go."

"Why should I not go to this house?" she asked, intrigued but not really mystified. In seeking a good riding horse, she had also made inquiries about the house set among the trees of the Oasis of Fadna. Word could have got about that she was going there to look at the house.

"You will go, *lella.*" Within the shadow of the hood the dark eyes gleamed again. "And you will go pursued by a man with dark hair."

She smiled and glanced up at fair-haired Rodney. "Well, that lets you out," she said lightly.

"Why, what did the old rascal say?" he demanded.

"Don't you speak French?" she asked.

"No, my own tongue is good enough for me!"

She quirked an eyebrow at his lack of humor. "I am told that I am being pursued by a man with dark hair," she said, a twinkle in her eyes.

11

"What absurd nonsense!" Rodney scowled and gave the Arab a look of scorn. "Give him a coin and come away, Lorna!"

"Not before I've heard some more—it might be nonsense, but it's amusing."

When she glanced again at the diviner, he at once bent intently over the sand patterns. "Who is this dark man?" she asked gaily. "Have I met him, or is he a stranger to me?"

"There are people whom we meet in dreams, *lella*. People who are strangers without being strange to us."

"I'm afraid I don't have dreams about tall, dark, dangerous men." She gave her rather cool and attractive laugh. "Can't you tell me something really interesting?"

"Has the *lella* no interest in the secrets of the heart?"

She detected a rather mocking note in the throaty voice, and an imp of defiance seized hold of her. With a triumphant smile she leant forward and blew the sand patterns out of shape. "There, now I have blown this dark man out of my path."

"No, *lella*." The sand-diviner indicated the hem of her blue silk dress, to which clung several grains of the fine sand. "The only way you can escape him is to leave the desert . . . if you stay you will be pursued until the hand of this man is upon you as the sand grains are."

The amusement died out of her eyes and she brushed the sand from her dress. It was foolish to take the game to heart, but all the same she felt suddenly cold and she fumbled with her beaded purse as she extracted a coin for the Arab. He took

12

it and stored it away in his robes. He gave her a *salaam* and murmured, *"Bilhana."*

"Shouldn't you warn me to beware?" she quipped, and then she turned hastily and suggested to Rodney that they hurry back to the ballroom for the last dance. The wailing of the Arab flute followed them, and she told herself she would be a fool to let the old fortune-teller disturb her. No one could read the future and it was just as well!

Half an hour ago she had run away from the noise and chatter of the hotel ball, but now she welcomed the music that drowned the sound of the flute.

"You dance awfully well," Rodney murmured, "yet you profess not to like dancing."

"I much prefer to ride," she said. "There's nothing to beat a gallop on a good horse—also I do the leading when I ride."

"So that's the reason?" His arm tightened about her. "You don't like being led by a man?"

"Not very much." She pulled out of his arms as the music died away and the dimmed lights began to brighten. Nearby a young man was kissing a girl on the ear, and Lorna gave the couple a cool look, almost as if she didn't understand the emotions that led to such an embrace.

"Goodnight, Rodney." She made for the door. "I expect to be up early, so I'm off to bed."

"Are you still set on riding alone in the desert?" he demanded, falling into step beside her.

"Of course." She gave him the same cool and inquiring look she had given the kissing couple. "Why should I change my plans?"

"The answer's obvious." He spoke in a low,

13

explosive tone as they reached the foot of the stairs. "You're too attractive to be here on your own, let alone in the desert. I shall come with you!"

"But I don't want you, Rodney." She stood on the stairs and looked down at him with cool blue eyes. "You would be in my way."

He flushed and his hand gripped the stair rail. "Have I been in your way all this week, then? Are you one of those frigid females who gets more fun out of her own company than that of a man?"

"I'm a little bit of a lone wolf," she admitted. "I'm sorry, Rodney, but I did warn you that I wasn't here to look for a husband in the tourist season. I am here just to suit myself, and I assure you I can look after myself. It's kind of you to offer your protection, but I'm not a helpless creature like Dolly Featherton."

Rodney gazed up at her, taking in her fair hair with its silvery sheen, her large blue eyes, and her slenderness in the blue silk dress. "If you aren't careful," he warned, "you'll meet your match and have some of that haughty coolness kissed out of you. Beware, Lorna! If you're made of ice, then the desert might melt you."

She laughed, and at that moment the Feathertons came out of the lounge. Plump Dolly with her permed hair and her pursed lips. Mrs. Featherton with her nose in the air. The husband, following behind the ladies, gave Lorna the usual greedy stare that his wife never saw because he was one of those men who had made a habit of doing things behind her back.

Lorna disliked the Feathertons, and with an airy wave at Rodney she went running up the stairs

14

to her suite. She supposed Rodney was right about her. She didn't like sharing herself with other people, though she was always the first to help anyone in trouble, especially a child or a suffering animal.

She switched on the light of her bedroom and walked over to the mirror. She studied her reflection and a wry little smile came and went on her lips. Rodney had accused her of a lack of feeling —but he meant the sort that responded to a careless caress or a passing kiss, and he was right in supposing that she had no desire to flirt with men. It wasn't coldness or lack of emotion. It was a total lack of interest in the kind of men she had met so far. They seemed so prosaic, so lacking in spirit and imagination.

Rodney had offered to ride with her in the desert, but she knew full well that he preferred diving in and out of the hotel swimming pool. Along with the other guests he seemed not to hear the call of the desert beyond the safe walls of the Ras Jusuf.

She prepared for bed, and lay beneath the netting with her thoughts full of the desert ride she planned to enjoy in the morning. Her entire being longed to see the sands as her father had seen them, a glowing, golden ocean of waves and hillocks that ran to meet the far horizon.

"It can be cruel and hot and menacing," her father had told her. "But there's beauty there, for those who can see it and appreciate it."

She thought also of the things the sand-diviner had said to her about the desert . . . that she would go to the house in the oasis pursued by a man.

It was absurd, but she was unable to control the shiver that ran over her, and like a little girl again she pulled the light covers over her head as if afraid of the darkness.

CHAPTER TWO

WEARING cream-colored breeches, a light shirt, and a slouch hat, Lorna made her way out of the hotel. A flask of coffee and a packet of biscuits were in the satchel in her hand, and her heart felt as light as the birds piping in the hedges of flowers as she made her way to the forecourt.

Already the sun was pink in the eastern sky, and her heartbeats quickened with excitement when she saw the stable boy, Ahmet, holding the reins of the horse she had hired from the local stables.

The boy grinned as she sauntered toward him, boyish in her breeches and open-necked shirt. "*Salaam aleikum.*" She tried out her Arabic as her gaze ran over the sleek chestnut who was snuffing the air and looking wonderfully fresh.

She tucked her biscuits and coffee-flask into the saddlebag and with an eager bound was in the saddle and grasping the reins. The boy gazed up at her, then burst out in broken French. "The boss says the *lella* must not go beyond the oasis, whose trees she will see just beyond the *hammada*. He says—"

"I know, Ahmet," she broke in with a laugh. "Like everyone else your boss will not hold himself responsible if I lose myself. Please tell him that I

17

don't intend to do anything foolish. I shall visit the oasis, and be back at the Ras Jusuf in time for lunch."

She gave the chestnut a prod of her heel and the next moment they were cantering beneath the archway that opened on to a quiet road, shaded by palms and leading to the open desert. At one side of the road ran the flower-hung wall of the hotel, at the other side a cool stream gradually petered out into a sandy *wadi*.

Lorna urged her mount across the *wadi* and almost at once the tangy desert air enveloped them. It was still so early that the day and the desert seemed to belong to her alone, and as she rode across the sands, the exhilaration she felt was far more potent than anything she had imagined.

Even the bazaars of the East had not thrilled her to this extent. Rambling and noisy, with dim alcoves in which silks glimmered, where iron was hammered, and perfumes distilled. Pungent and picturesque, even mysterious. Lorna had enjoyed the many aromas, and exploring the sudden flights of stairs, and buying odd mementos of her visit . . . but here in the desert she felt much closer to the eternal mystery of the East.

She brought her mount to a halt and gazed around at the long, smooth combers of sand. The sun seemed trapped in the waves of amber and burnt gold, and crystals glittered among the grains like scattered gems. The wind across the open spaces had polished the sandstone boulders and they had a reddish tinge, while overhead the sky was unbelievably blue.

Allah's golden garden, where travelers sought

peace of heart, adventure . . . or their destiny.

Lorna was unsure what she was seeking. She knew only that she was restless and lonely since losing her father. She hoped this sojourn in the desert might give her some sense of direction . . . she had thought of becoming a nurse, but first she had to get the desert out of her system. She had to touch the dream and then perhaps it might let her go.

Ahead of her lay the sweeping ridge of the *hammada,* and she let the chestnut break into a gallop and felt the wind in her face as they neared the uplands that hid from view the palm trees of the oasis.

Without pause or effort the horse bounded up the slopes of rock, and Lorna felt quite unafraid as they climbed higher and higher, until the desert sands lay shimmering far beneath them. Now the sun was burning overhead and Lorna felt the heat. There was a water-bottle in the saddlebag and she paused to take a drink. Then she pulled her slouch hat over her eyes and sat firm in the saddle as the chestnut picked his way down to the other side of the *hammada* and with the loping strides of an Arabian horse made for the blessed green tufts that indicated the Oasis of Fadna.

Lorna dismounted beneath the cool shade of the trees and took off her hat, which left her hair clinging damply to her temples and her nape. Mmm, what a relief to be out of the sun! She heard a cooing of pigeons and went eagerly forward to get a glimpse of the house, upon which the birds must be nesting.

There wasn't another sound except for that

cooing. It was as if the oasis held its breath; as if it awaited the pained cry that broke from Lorna as she came in sight of what was left of the house in which her father had lived and painted.

The small, whitewashed building was now a crumbling ruin, overrun by some sort of flowering weed that sought to hide the broken walls among the dateless palms of the oasis.

Lorna slumped against a palm tree and gazed in disappointment at what was left of her dream . . . and in that moment the words of the sand-diviner were vividly real. He had said that the sands had encroached upon the house and smothered the flowers once planted along its walls, and because her dream of living here awhile had been so alive, it was even more shocking that the house should be so dead.

If Lorna had been a girl who wept easily, she might have wept for the passing of her dream. She knew that another house could be built here, but it wouldn't be the same. Its air and its atmosphere would not be those of the father she had loved and lost.

She turned away from the ruin and plucked a white flower that had clung tenaciously to life and bloomed on the broken wall, and she did not look back as she made her way among the trees to where she had left her horse. Now the oasis seemed shadowed, and she wanted to ride away and let the sands set lightly on the spirit of her wise and witty father. Only a rose-like flower was left of his presence, and she tucked it into the pocket of her shirt.

She came to the edge of the oasis and glanced

about for her mount. His tracks were deep in the sand, but the chestnut himself was nowhere to be seen!

Lorna whistled and went running among the trees in search of him, and as a sense of panic mounted in her, she realized that in her eagerness to look at the house she had failed to tether the horse. She had forgotten that he was not Gige, her faithful mount back in France who followed her about like a great dog and needed no tether. The chestnut was an Arab horse. Finding himself free he had galloped off and left her to face a long walk back to the hotel, across the sands and the rocky *hammada*.

The prospect was daunting, and again if she had been the weeping sort she might have wept at her own heedlessness. Her coffee-flask and biscuits were in the saddlebag of the horse, along with the water-bottle. Her only consolation was that a small stream watered the oasis and she would not go thirsty while she waited for the sun to cool down. It would be madness to attempt the long walk while the desert sun was high; only in the cool of the evening would it be wise to set out for the Ras Jusuf.

"You ass, Lorna!" She threw herself down in the shade of a palm tree and tipped her hat over her eyes so she could gaze out across the sands in the forlorn hope that the chestnut would come trotting back.

The pigeons still cooed, but there wasn't a flutter of a leaf. It was noon, when the sun reached its zenith and shone with brutal strength for several hours. When it began to set a chill would creep over the desert and Lorna's trek would be cold and lonely, with queer shadows lurking in the hollows of the sand dunes.

She dug her booted heels into the sand and settled down for a long wait. As yet she wasn't nervous, only annoyed with herself for being so careless. The chestnut would return to the stables from which she had borrowed him, and everyone at the hotel would have the satisfaction of saying that a girl like herself wasn't to be trusted alone in the desert.

She wrinkled her nose as she thought of the Feathertons, and shrugged a slim shoulder as she remembered Rodney's warning. "Girls have been carried off and never heard of again!"

She trickled sand through her fingers and was certain that no Arab would find her slender proportions to his taste. Arabs liked their women plump and submissive, and she gave a laugh at the thought of ever being submissive to a man. She was amazed by the girls who couldn't wait to be fettered to one by a wedding ring. She couldn't help but love her own freedom.

Mmm, a cigaret would be welcome right now, but in her eagerness to rise and ride she had left her cigaret-case and her lighter on the dressing table of the hotel bedroom.

She rested her head against the trunk of the palm tree and drowsed for a while, until the longing for a cup of coffee became so tormenting that she rose to her feet and made for the stream that wended its way among the trees. She knelt and assuaged her thirst and dabbed the cool water against her temples. Drops of it ran down her neck and made her flimsy apricot shirt cling to her. She eyed the surrounding trees and wished they were date palms, hung with great bunches of glistening amber fruit.

And then all at once she stiffened and felt a stirring of unease . . . a sense that she was not alone in the oasis. The feeling held her immobile for chilling seconds, and then she leaped to her feet and swung round.

Her senses had not misled her . . . a robed figure was standing among the trees staring at her. He was swarthy, bearded, and even as Lorna looked at him with alarm he unwound a scarf from about his throat and began to approach her in a stealthy, purposeful way.

"What do you want?" she cried out.

A pair of cunning eyes stared into hers and Lorna realized that he *wanted her.* She turned to flee, and then cried out in pain and horror as a long arm reached out and dark fingers caught her by the hair. The dirty white scarf was flung over her face, throttling the scream that rose in her throat. Again and yet again the scarf was bound about her mouth and with a sense of nightmare she felt her hands gripped behind her and secured in the long ends of the scarf.

She kicked, struggled, made a brave effort to run and was tripped on her face and then jerked roughly to her feet. Again those mean little eyes held hers, then the Arab jerked her into a walk, past the shell of the house and out under the trees at the other side of the oasis, where a fine black horse stood flicking its long tail at the sand flies.

The stallion was tethered to a tree and as Lorna was pushed toward him, he shied in a nervous way and she saw the rowel marks where spurs had been used on him. There were spurs on the Arab's boots and his hands were equally cruel as he threw her across the withers of the horse and then leaped into the scarlet saddle.

The horse jibbed, reared up, and gave a shrill neigh as the Arab jerked roughly on the reins, directing the animal away from the *hammada* toward the open desert.

Lorna's heart was gripped by fear and panic, for now the Arab had thrown his *burnous* over her and was holding her against him as the stallion bounded forward across the sands. It was a brutal, bruising grip, and the blinding folds of the *burnous* made it impossible for her to see, or to breathe properly. Her head was spinning, she could hardly think straight. . . ."

This brute had followed her to the oasis, and it was all too horribly true what Rodney had said about desert kidnappers. She should have listened to him, but wilful and sure of herself she had dismissed his warning as nonsense. She had invited something like this to happen by her own stubbornness, but hadn't for a moment dreamed that it would!

Where was the brute taking her?

She could feel the speed of the stallion, and it struck her as strange that so beautiful an animal should belong to her bearded abductor. In all probability it didn't. Someone who was low enough to kidnap a girl wouldn't hesitate to steal a horse.

On and on raced the stallion, with only a short pause while the Arab took a drink from his water-bottle. He offered none to Lorna, but she heard the gurgle of the water as he drank and took the opportunity to wriggle her head free of the musky *burnous*.

The desert stretched all around them, a sea of silence and burning sand, which weighed upon her shocked senses and gave her the feeling that she was lost to her only friend at the Ras Jusuf . . . the young man who would have been with her at the Oasis of Fadna if she had not rejected him with scornfully unkind words. Now she longed for him to come . . . prayed for someone to end this nightmare!

The stallion started forward again, and the Arab's arm securely imprisoned Lorna against the none-too-clean robes. Now and again he growled to himself as if he were feeling the heat, and perhaps a certain impatience. He spurred the stallion and Lorna felt the quiver that ran over the fine animal. It wasn't used to such treatment!

Lorna was drooping with fatigue and seeing everything through a haze when a band of horsemen appeared suddenly, strung out in a line upon a high, sweeping ridge of sand, like figures in an etching, or a dream. The sun was behind them and they raced darkly against the vivid glow, their cloaks flying out above the hindquarters of their mounts.

As they swooped with precision down the hill of sand, Lorna's abductor checked his mount for a moment and she heard him mutter something in his throat. Then he swung the stallion away from the cloaked riders and put him into a gallop that threw Lorna closer still to the beastly robes. He was afraid of the horsemen, and at once her heart bounded with the hope that they had run into a desert patrol.

She craned her neck to get a look at the horsemen and saw that one of them was riding well ahead of the others. His mount was as black and sleek as her kidnapper's, but there was extra speed in him because he carried only a single burden, a dark-robed figure which crouched over the saddle and held something in his right hand.

Lorna thought it was a gun, and then as the distance shortened between them she saw him draw back his hand and let fly with the object. There was a raw whine and something snaked darkly about the Arab who held her . . . He let out a cry, let go of Lorna and went toppling out of the saddle. At the same instant the cloaked rider drew alongside the stallion and Lorna was snatched from his back before she could be thrown.

Stunned, breathless, she heard a deep call of command that sent the stallion spinning high on its back legs, then it came to a panting halt, its flanks heaving, its body streaming with sweat.

The other riders galloped up. Lorna, still very confused, was handed over to one of them like a doll. Their leader then dismounted with a wide flare of his cloak and approached the misused stallion. He gentled him and spoke soothingly in a deep, soft voice. He examined the raked legs, and then he swung round and never in her life had Lorna seen a face so striking, so fierce, so stamped with autocracy. His lips were drawn into a thin line as he strode to the Arab he had unseated with a horsewhip. Deliberately that whip was raised and

26

Lorna was held speechless as her kidnapper was soundly flogged.

Then the tall, cloaked figure turned to Lorna who felt a thrill of fear like no other as she met the man's tawny eyes. Eyes that glittered and commanded and were made extra startling by the black lashes that surrounded them and the black level brows that bridged them.

He flashed those tawny eyes over her from head to foot and in a stride he came to her and unwound the scarf from about her face. She took a deep gulp of air and blinked her sweat-tangled lashes. She couldn't speak for several seconds, for everything had happened so suddenly.

"I'm grateful to you, *m'sieu*," she said in French, but her voice shook and her gratitude was unsure. She gestured at the Arab, beaten into a huddled heap on the sands. "He carried me off— for money I think."

"Money, eh?" The tawny eyes lingered on the sunlit confusion of her hair. A soft wave flopped forward, framing her deep blue eyes; her neck rose slim and white out of the opening of her shirt. "Not content with stealing horses, he steals a *petite fille*! He has been a busy fellow."

Lorna knew flawless French when she heard it spoken, but somehow it seemed strange coming from a man who wore a desert cloak, a headcloth bound by a dark cord, and tall boots of polished leather.

"The horse is mine." The gesture he made toward the tired stallion was very Gallic. "*Mon Dieu,* I did not think to get him back with a bonus!"

Suddenly the man smiled, his fine teeth flashing

white against the sun-bronzed skin of his lean face. A smile usually had the effect of softening a face, but this man's features remained forceful, striking, and a devilish glint came into his eyes. He looked illimitably sure of himself and far from in need of ransom money . . . Lorna's heart began to pound in the most alarming fashion.

"I am called Kasim ben Hussayn." He gave her a slight foreign bow. "May I know the name of the *petite Anglaise*? Come, tell me!"

She gave a nervous start at the imperious click of his fingers, and there swept over her a feeling of wanting to tell him to mind his own business . . . whatever that might be!

"I am Lorna Morel," she said in her coolest tones. "I would be grateful if one of your men could escort me back to the Ras Jusuf Hotel at Yraa, where I am staying. He will be generously paid for his trouble."

"He will, eh?" A disconcerting glint came into the tawny eyes. "What in your estimation is suitable payment for rescuing a foolish girl from the hands of a horse thief? A handful of francs?"

She was held by eyes that reflected the color of the desert and even as she disliked him for mocking her, she thought again that he spoke like a Frenchman and used his hands in a Gallic way. Her father had been friendly with French people during the year they had lived in Paris—the last year of his life—and a couple of the men had tried to overcome her reserve with their Gallic charm. She had been amused by them, but they had got no further than a kiss on her wrist.

"I am tired and thirsty, *m'sieu,* and not in the

mood for riddles." She brushed the soft wave of hair out of her eyes. "May I have a guide to take me to the hotel?"

"Are you not going to thank me for coming to your rescue?"

"I did—in the beginning."

"Because you thought me a French officer in charge of a desert patrol." He tossed his cloak over his shoulder with an arrogant gesture. "Do I look a Frenchman, *mademoiselle?*"

She thought he looked as arrogant as the devil. "I should so like a drink of water," she said huskily.

He said something to one of his men, who leaped at once from his horse and approached the black stallion. He took the reins and climbed into the scarlet saddle. Lorna made an instinctive movement of retreat as the picturesque figure who gave the orders took a step toward her. He caught at the scarf that bound her hands and released them, and the breath seemed to get lost in her throat as he took hold of her and tossed her into the saddle of the vacated horse.

"Drink!" He gestured at the water-bottle that hung from the pommel of the horse's saddle. "We have a long ride ahead of us."

She gulped gratefully at the water, then closed the leather top and hung the bottle by its strap on the high-peaked saddle. "I don't need an entire escort, *m'sieu.*" Her smile was faintly nervous. "One man will do, just to show me the way to the hotel."

"The hotel?" He quirked a black eyebrow. "We are not going to Yraa . . . we are returning to my encampment."

Lorna gazed wildly, unbelievingly at the man. She watched speechlessly as he leaped into the saddle of his horse, his cloak like a dark wing about him. Her hands were slack on the reins of her mount as she took in the meaning of his words . . . he was not taking her to the hotel but to his camp! He was abducting her, and certainly not for ransom! His clothes, his entourage, his entire manner proclaimed him as someone of importance . . . one look at his men was enough to tell her that they were trained to the eyebrows to obey him. His will was theirs!

They were trained to obey his slightest whim, but she wasn't! Digging her heels into her horse's flanks she broke through their ranks and galloped madly away. She wasn't giving in tamely to any man, least of all that tall, mocking devil with eyes as tawny as the desert sands.

CHAPTER THREE

HE allowed her to get ahead of him for about a mile, then with superb ease he rode her down, swooped in close, like a hawk on its prey, encircled her with his arm and swept her in front of him.

As she felt his touch, as she heard him laugh, she began to fight him with a desperation almost primitive, punching his shoulders, wishing she had fingernails long enough to claw out his eyes. His teeth were a flash of white against his bronze skin, and with his knees alone he gripped and guided his horse until he had Lorna bound firmly in the folds of his cloak.

She lay panting across his saddlebow, bruised by his hands, hot and dizzy with rage and hate. "You brute!" The words broke from her. "What do you think you are doing?"

"I should think the answer was obvious—go gently, Caliph!" He addressed his horse, alarmed by the struggle that had just taken place on its back. "We have a little wildcat with us—yes, *ma fille,* you would have my eyes if you could get at them, eh?"

He laughed down into Lorna's eyes and he subdued her as if she were no more than a child with a child's strength. "Little fool, you have fatigued yourself all for nothing . . . do you think Kasim ben Hussayn is to be overcome by a wisp of a girl?"

He touched the wave of hair above her eyes and subjected her to a look that chased the angry color out of her cheeks. "Tell me, is your hair truly this color?" It was a look not of mere admiration, such as she was used to, but that of a man who took what he desired and begged for nothing.

"Soie sauvage." He gazed fascinated at the silvery-gold strand of hair he wound about his brown hand. "Wild silk, golden as the desert itself."

Lorna shrank from him as far as possible. "You . . . you flogged that other man for stealing a horse!" Her blue eyes held a terror she had never known before. This man frightened her far more than the bearded Arab who had carried her away from the oasis. It made no difference that the cloak around her was clean as the desert air and faintly redolent of Turkish tobacco — an aroma she recognized because her father had smoked such cigarets. It didn't help that the lean hands that subdued her were clean as his robes. His very handsomeness made her go cold.

"My horses are valuable to me and I won't have them stolen and misused." He gazed down into Lorna's eyes and she was reminded of a leopard, arrogant and sure of other people's fear of him. "I never grow tired of my horses. They are beautiful, voiceless, and loyal. Can the same be said for many women?"

As his horse bounded forward into the flamy light that was spreading across the desert, his men fell into rank behind him. Lorna closed her eyes to shut out his face above her, then she opened them again and tried to read in the bronzed features some sign of mercy . . . but there was none.

This was real and not a nightmare. She lay doubly imprisoned by the folds of his dark cloak and his strong arm. She felt the movements of the horse, but in her tired state was only half-aware when the sun died in a blaze of color and night fell quickly, purple-shadowed beneath the Arabian stars.

It was a strange lullaby, the clinking of bridles and the silver adorning them, and some time later the rhythm of the riders altered and Lorna stirred out of the strange dream into which she had fallen . . . and found that it was nighttime.

She was wrapped more comfortably in the great riding cloak, and the Shaikh and his men had come to a standstill in a moonlit encampment of black tents. She saw the kneeling shapes of camels, and the glow of camp fires. She heard voices speaking in Arabic, and still confused she was lifted to the ground. She felt stiff, and was only vaguely aware of the exotic wonder of the night and the vibrations of the big camp all around her.

She trembled, but not with cold. Overhead the moon was a sickle of gold, and the profile of her captor was outlined against the moonlit sky as he gave orders to his men in deep, commanding Arabic, not a word of which she understood.

Then abruptly he turned to Lorna. She saw the arrogant smile on his lips and torn between fury and fear she awoke out of her dream state and lifting a hand she struck him across the face. Once . . . twice . . . needing an outlet for the terror he

33

awoke in her, hoping he would break her neck.

But he only laughed deep in his throat and swung her up into his arms. The people watched, their faces like golden masks in the firelight, as he strode with her to the great tent that stood in splendid isolation beyond the ring of camp fires.

With a thrust of his shoulder he opened the flap of the tent and strode inside with her, his booted feet abruptly silenced on the deep pile of the carpets that covered the floor. He stood holding her a prisoner. She sustained his arrogant gaze, though it weakened her and frightened her.

"You barbarian!" she raged. "If you think you can get away with this, then you're in for a surprise. I'm a British subject!"

"Undoubtedly," he rejoined lazily. "I am on my own territory and subject to no one but myself. Tell me, my spitfire, what do I intend to get away with?"

His look mocked her, and she saw every detail of his face in the light from the brass lamps that emitted an aroma of sandalwood. The outer corners of his eyes had a faint slant to them; the sculpturing of his brow and his nose was faultless; his nostrils were tempered, and his jawline had a clean, hard sweep to it.

She looked at his mouth . . . imperiously quirked in a smile that took no heed of her feelings.

"I have money." There was a note of torment in her voice. "You can have it if you let me go!"

He answered with a soft laugh and dropped her to her feet. "I have no need of your money, so I fear it cannot buy your freedom. There is only one thing that can, and you are surpassingly innocent if you don't know what it is."

She stared at him, her eyes like bruised flowers in her pale, shocked face. "I don't know," she whispered.

"Really?" His eyes flicked over her. "With your unusual looks, you tell me you don't know what a man means when he brings you to his tent. *Ma belle femme,* I think you do know."

And as the words sank into her brain, she backed away from him until brought up short by a divan. She drew his cloak about her slim body and gazed around wildly for some means of escape from him. There was a beaded partition that led into another part of the sumptuous tent, but directly Lorna's gaze fell upon it, she realized with a thump of her heart that it was the *harem* section of his tent.

As her desperate glance united again with his and she saw the smile glimmering deep in his eyes, she said with icy fury, "I'm not a *fille de joie!* I am here in the East on holiday and when I'm found to be missing a search will be made for me. You will be punished if I come to . . . to any sort of harm."

"The tryrant trembles!" He took a stride forward and whipped the cloak away from her, leaving her revealed in her flimsy open-necked shirt and boyish breeches. Never had she been looked at so brazenly. Never had she been so aware of being an attractive female.

"A girl such as you should not be allowed to wander alone like a gipsy," he said, and his gaze was on the sensitive curve of her lips. "It is a folly to be young, eh? To follow the impulse rather than take notice of those who are wiser? I am sure you were warned that the desert could be . . .

dangerous. I am equally sure that you took no heed of the warning. How very rash of you."

A shiver ran over her, for each deliberate word was like the tip of a lash laying bare the fear in her heart. She drew back with a gasp as he curved a hand around the nape of her neck and forced her to look at him. "You are lovely as golden gorse and as thorny to the touch—in a symbolic sense," he added with a smile, his gaze on the soft slim line of her throat. "You don't like a man to touch you, eh? Where have you been to acquire such coolness—in a convent?"

"You . . . you needed to go nowhere to acquire your cruelty," she choked. "You are a devil!"

"I am merely a man." His smile was slow, dangerous, showing the edge of his white teeth. "I believe that everything hinges on fate and I would no more argue with *le destin* than I would with a sand cat. Fate has thrown us together—*comprenez-vous?*"

"I understand only one thing," her heart beat frantically as she gazed up into the face that was so ruthlessly handsome. "You will not only dishonor me if you keep me here."

"I cannot be moved by that plea." His hand moved to her shoulder and she felt his touch right through the thin material of her shirt. "What has honor to do with what a man feels for a woman?" He laughed and bent his tall head and laid a kiss against her throat. "How swiftly your pulse beats. Are you so afraid of me?"

"I hate you!" So soft a kiss, yet how it lingered, as if a flame had touched her . . . as if always she would be marked. "I think you're despicable!"

36

"You I find utterly exciting." He held her so that she was like a plant leaning back before an unrelenting wind. "Your hair is like the gold of the desert sun, your eyes are the color of blue jasmine, and your skin is pale like a desert dawn. I want you, my flower of blue and gold, and I prefer what I take to what I am given."

"You can't mean . . . ?" Her words died away and left only a speechless imploration in her eyes.

"You know that I mean every word." He laughed softly. "Women are all instinct—your instinct must surely tell you why I bring you to my tent."

He stroked her hair, ran caressing fingers across her throat, and then when she tried to break away from him, when she again fought with him, he gripped her cruelly, crushed her to him, revealed the strength that could have broken her in two.

"Beauty and spirit," he smiled, uncaring that he bruised her. "A little tiger-kitten who has not yet been tamed. *Très bien,* we shall fight and afterwards—afterwards we shall kiss."

With these words he let her go and swung on his heel. He strode from the tent and as the flap fell into place behind him, Lorna sank down exhausted on a divan and buried her face in her hands. She was trembling from head to foot, but the relief of tears was denied to her. There was no weeping away the knowledge that she had fallen into the hands of a man who made his own laws and was quite ruthless . . . ruthless and handsome in a way she had not associated with men of the East.

Those she had seen in the bazaars had been obese or hungry-looking. This man was princely to look at . . . an autocrat like those in ancient stories of Harun al Raschid and his pagan court.

What made it worse was that in her own arrogance she had not listened to Rodney Grant when he had warned her not to ride alone in the desert. Rodney had warned . . . the sand-diviner had seen the writing in the sand . . . but wilful, restless, wanting no rein but that of the father she had lost, she had let the desert lure her into its golden coils.

The start she gave as someone quietly entered the tent was proof of the shaken state of her nerves. She glanced up wildly, not a tinge of color in her cheeks, as her eyes dwelt on a manservant with a snowy turban encircling his head. He touched a hand to forehead, eyes and lips to indicate that each was at her service.

"Water is being brought so the *lella* can bathe," he said in excellent French, "and also a change of clothing. My master will then eat supper with his— guest."

That slight, significant pause before the word brought back to Lorna's cheeks the color that had fled from them. She jumped to her feet and said desperately "I must get away from here! If you will provide me with a horse, I'll pay you most generously—"

"The money would be worthless to me, *madame.*" The manservant backed away from her. "My master would punish me within an inch of my life!"

With a bow he retreated from the tent, and Lorna realized forlornly that there probably wasn't a soul in the camp who would dare risk the Shaikh's displeasure.

She pressed a hand to her throat, feeling the place where he had kissed her. The memory of it, so recent and burning, sent her running through the bead curtain into the interior room of the tent . . . the *harem*.

She gazed around and saw that it was furnished with a low, wide ottoman overlaid by a gold silk coverlet embroidered with blue jasmine flowers. Beside the bed stood an inlaid table holding a lamp, a cigaret-box, and a brass matchbox. Lorna ran the tip of her tongue round her dry lips. Her nerves cried out for a cigaret, and thrusting aside the thought that they were *his*, she knelt on the bed and reached for one.

They were Turkish but she was too much in need of a smoke to care. She struck a match and carried the flame to the tip. The first draw was a trifle harsh, but after a moment or two quite soothing. She sat there on the bed, fatigued and yet tensed for every movement, every sound, taking in the luxurious trappings of her captor's *harem*.

A tawny leopard skin was spread across the carpets. The brass oil-lamps emitted the faint pervasiveness of sandalwood, and there was a lacquered chest on which stood a mirror and the toiletries of a man.

This room, like the person of the Shaikh, was spotlessly clean. The sumptuous hangings and the huge pillows were without a mark, and across the foot of the ottoman lay a black silk robe and a pair of pajamas to match.

Lorna felt the nervous beating of her heart as

she shrank away from the masculine night attire. The intimacy of the room struck at her like a talon. Here *he* slept. Here he relaxed at the end of the day and read the books with French titles grouped in a bookcase beside the bed.

She stubbed the cigaret, and every nerve in her body seemed to shrink as the bead curtain opened to let in a veiled young woman.

"I am Zahra." The girl stared curiously at Lorna, taking in her fair hair and boyish riding clothes. She released her veil, then darted back through the partition to return a minute later carrying a pair of steaming copper kettles. These she set down on a knee-high table, and swishing aside a brocade curtain she revealed an alcove in which stood a circular, deep-sided copper bowl, large enough for a person to bathe in.

"The *lella* wishes to take a bath?" The girl spoke broken French.

Lorna longed to take one. She nodded and the girl filled the bathing bowl from the two big kettles, then she took bath towels from a carved chest and poured scented bath-oil into the water. The stream arose, aromatic and inviting, and it was a relief to Lorna when the pretty creature slipped through the beaded curtain, smiling to indicate that she was off to fetch something else.

Lorna stripped off her dusty clothes and stepped into the bowl, which was large enough for her to kneel in. She washed herself all over with the scented soapy water, and was wrapped in one of the huge towels when Aahra returned, carrying some flimsy garments over her arm. She showed each one to Lorna, a shift so fine it was transparent, silk

40

trousers with embroidery around the ankles, a velvet tunic, and a pair of dove-soft slippers with uptilted toes.

Lorna gazed at the garments with scorn in her eyes. It was a *harem* outfit!

"No." She shook her head firmly at the girl, who at once looked bewildered and a trifle nervous. "Quite definitely no." Lorna turned aside from Zahra and began to don her own clothes; the boyish breeches and boots that made her feel a little armored against the Shaikh. She buttoned with shaking fingers the apricot-colored shirt that was so unfeminine beside the garments he had ordered to be brought to her.

She was no *harem* girl. Frightened of him though she was, she would not submit without a fight.

She tilted her chin and met Zahra's great brown eyes. *"Je suis désolée."* She shrugged her shoulders. "I cannot wear those things—*comprenez?"*

The girl studied them and was plainly at a loss to understand the *lella's* reluctance to wear such appealing garments. "The Prince Kasim will be angry," she said in awe, in her attractive broken French.

"Prince!" Lorna looked scornful. "I hope I make him angry enough to break my neck."

She swung around to the mirror that stood on the lacquered chest and saw that her hair was untidy. With reluctance she picked up the tortoiseshell comb and pulled it through the tangles in her hair. She always carried a lipstick in her pocket and as she applied it a bitter little smile curled her

41

lips. War paint. Woman's eternal weapon in times of crisis.

When she turned from the mirror she saw that Zahra had slipped away. The silk and velvets lay in a colorful, flimsy heap on a hassock, the scarlet slippers beside them.

"I wouldn't be seen dead in them!" Lorna whispered fiercely, and then because the *harem* had become unendurable she slipped through the bead curtain into the main part of the tent. She stared at the knee-high table that had been set for two in front of a divan heaped with cushions. There were pearl-handled cutlery and silver-rimmed glasses, adding to Lorna's sense of antagonism.

The man who had brought her to his tent was a handsome, merciless devil who lived liked a prince. She bit her lip. He was exactly that, according to Zahra. An arrogant prince . . . soon to come sweeping into the tent, tall and tawny-eyed.

CHAPTER FOUR

LORNA gazed around the tent, with its mingling aromas of leather, sandalwood and horses. The interior walls were hung with tapestry, and the lamps lent a lambent glow to the simple luxury of the furnishings. The carpets were Kashan, she was sure of it. And there was an ebony table on which stood a beautifully carved box.

She went and opened the box and a gasp of astonishment escaped her. It contained an ivory chess set and so exquisitely carved were the pieces they were almost transparent. Lorna, who had been taught some of the rudiments of the game by her father, picked up an intricate knight and was admiring it when there was a slight movement behind her.

She swung round, clutching the knight, and the blood seemed to drain from her heart.

The Shaikh had entered in his silent way and he stood with his back to the flat of the tent. He had removed his riding outfit and wore a slash-throated *kibr* encircled by a waistband. His black, close-cut hair was uncovered, and there was a leopard grace and assurance about the man as he stood looking at her . . . taking in the breeches and boots she had refused to discard.

43

His eyelids narrowed, and she tensed herself for battle.

"Do you play chess?" he asked.

She had fully expected him to ask why she wasn't wearing the change of clothing he had provided, and she felt the tremor in her hand as she returned the chess-piece to the carved box. As she closed the lid she said coldly, "Do you play, *m'sieu?*"

"Such games of advance and retreat were invented by the subtle mind of the East," he drawled, and as he moved toward her, she tensed, a slim creature wanting to streak for cover.

"You are as nervous as a sand bird." He bent to take a nut from a dish on the table, an almond which he crushed between his strong teeth. The white tunic he wore accentuated the sunburned skin of his face, throat, and arms. On the forefinger of his right hand Lorna noticed a heavy ring engraved with golden characters. He was so darkly handsome, so overwhelming, with such wide and easily carried shoulders, that he seemed to cast a shadow around Lorna as he towered over her, his back to the lamplight.

"You look at me as if I mean to eat you," he taunted. "Why are you not wearing the things I told the girl to bring you? Surely you would feel more comfortable if you discarded those riding breeches and boots?"

"I prefer to stay as I am!" She dug her hands into the pockets of her breeches and assumed a boyish stance. "Why send me the clothes, Prince Kasim? Would it ease your conscience to see me dressed like a *harem* girl?"

He quirked a black eyebrow. "When I am in camp I prefer the title of Shaikh—apart from which, as you must know, the devil has no conscience."

"Have you strings of titles?" she asked scornfully. "To me you are worse than that horse thief! He was poor and out for the money when he . . . kidnapped me."

"What makes you so certain of that?" Once again the white teeth crushed a nut between them.

"Because to an ordinary Arab I must seem pale and stringy," she said with spirit. "Not the admired moon of full curves, with the eyes of a gazelle."

The Shaikh laughed softly . . . it was like a purring deep in his brown throat. "You are very modest for a female, and no doubt you wish that I found you pale and stringy." His tawny eyes slipped over her. "I am disappointed that you choose to wear those boy's clothes. I think Eastern garments look at their best on a lissome figure."

When he mentioned her figure, in that deep, deliberate voice, Lorna wanted to run and hide herself. She felt suddenly that the apricot shirt clung to her, that the boyish breeches revealed the slenderness of her hips. Her relief was beyond words when the flap of the tent opened and the Shaikh's servant carried in a tray on which were several dome-covered dishes.

With deft hands he arranged the dishes on the table, and he poured into the silver-rimmed glasses a liquid that shimmered cool and green. Not once did he glance at Lorna. His eyes were discreetly lowered as he bowed and withdrew from the tent, leaving her alone with his master.

"Please be seated." The Shaikh gestured at the divan.

"I . . . I'm not hungry," she said defiantly.

"I am sure you are, *mon enfant.*" He lifted her as if she were a child and settled her among the big cushions of the divan. He sat down beside her and handed her one of the glasses. "This is limoon, a drink of crushed limes, wild mint, and a little honey. Come, I know you are thirsty."

"You know nothing about me," she rejoined. "To you I am only an object!"

"A very decorative one." He put the rim of the glass to her lips and his voice softened. "You are foolish and a little wilful, like a filly who sees her reflection in a pool and shies away from the image. Don't you care for your own beauty?"

Lorna looked at him with eyes that were purely violet in that moment; eyes that looked as if someone had plucked two flowers and pressed them into her pale young face.

"Drink," the Shaikh softly commanded. "Your voice is husky when you speak, and I don't wish to force your compliance."

"Force is all you know!" she flung at him. "Your own people are terrified of you."

"What makes you say that? Did you find Zahra and Hassan reluctant to help you escape?" He laughed, and because he was so near to her, holding the glass of limoon to her lips, she took it and drew away from him. She sipped at the drink, and watched him tearing apart with sunburned fingers the roasted quails that topped the dish of beautifully cooked rice and vegetables.

"Come, you must eat, but I don't expect you to

eat with your fingers." He indicated the pearl-handled cutlery. "You have been out in the desert air most of the day and must be feeling hungry. Hassan is a superb cook and he will be hurt if he finds you have not tasted a morsel of our supper."

Our supper. She shuddered, but because the Shaikh's tawny eyes were upon her, she took some of the *cous-cous* and forced herself to eat it.

"Some quail as well," he coaxed, laying one of the roasted birds on her plate.

"It's typical of you to like quail," she said, knowing the quails were netted in the desert for their tenderness.

"All the same," he looked at her and quirked an eyebrow in typical fashion, "you will admit that they make a meal fit for a king."

"A prince," she corrected him, and she looked deliberately at the way he rolled the *cous-cous* neatly in the fingers of his right hand and popped the ball in his mouth. Lorna had the feeling that he ate like a desert man on purpose, and when she heard him laugh she knew she was right.

Hassan returned in a while with their coffee, which he poured into small cups in filigreed holders. It was French coffee, but in her fear and her apprehension Lorna could not fully enjoy it. The Shaikh said something to Hassan before he departed, and the quickened beat of Lorna's heart told her that from now on they would be left alone.

It surprised her when the flap of the tent was opened once more to permit entrance to a long-legged silky-coated gazelle hound, which bounded across the tent and settled its front paws upon the shoulders of the man beside her.

47

He ruffled the coat of the animal with a fond hand, and glanced at Lorna. "Do you care for dogs?" he asked. "British people are usually sentimental about them."

"Yes, I like dogs," she replied, but she eyed the *saluki* with the same distrust with which she looked at his master. The dog eyed her, and then came to sniff at her boots.

"There is no need to be nervous of Fedjr," said the Shaikh, as he lounged back against the cushions of the divan. "He's far more gallant than I am, being a true son of the desert."

Lorna didn't fully understand what he meant. To her, in every respect, he was the desert at its most dangerous, its most subtle, its most picturesque. Without any real fear she held out a hand to Fedjr and found his muzzle cool and soft. He snuffed her fingers, and his master gave a deep, soft laugh as the hound rested his handsome head on her knee and gazed up soulfully into her face.

"You are a novelty to him." The Shaikh leaned forward and took a cigaret from the box at his elbow. "Will you smoke, Lorna?"

He spoke her name with the accent on the R so that it was almost a deep purr . . . the very fact that he used her name so intimately made her furious.

"No thank you! They're a brand to which I'm not accustomed."

"One can grow used to what at first seems alien," he said, a meaning glint in his eyes as he struck a match and wedded the flame to his cigaret. He exhaled smoke, and his gaze dwelt lazily on Lorna as she stroked the hound. She could not relax. She felt the man's power and energy far more

48

potently than if he had been a person who prowled about a room.

"Of what are you thinking?" he demanded.

"Of a friend at the hotel at Yraa, who will be extremely worried about me." Her voice shook and her lashes made dramatic little shadows on her cheekbones.

"Is this friend a man?" There was the whisper of a lash in the question.

"Of course." She glanced up and met his eyes with appeal and defiance in her own eyes. "He will organize a search for me—he knew I was going to the Oasis of Fadna, and he will hire Arab trackers to find me."

"They will need to be keen-eyed," he said sardonically. "Each morning, after the caress of the night winds, the sands of the desert are virgin again."

"Rodney will find me!" The words broke in desperation from her.

"He is fond of you, eh, this man called Rodney?" The cigaret smoke drifted blue-tinged beside the eyes that were desert-tawny . . . leopard-lazy.

"He . . . he's very fond of me." She shut her mind to her careless rejection of Rodney Grant. "I . . . I'm sure you have no use, *m'sieu,* for a woman who belongs already to another man."

"A man who allowed you to go alone into the desert?" The tawny eyes roved her hair, her face, and came to rest on the pulse that beat visibly beneath the soft skin of her throat. "The desert is a place to be shared and I don't believe, *ma fille,* that you wished to share its magic with this man."

"We . . . we had an argument and I rode off in a huff without him. . . ."

"Did he give chase?" The eyes that dwelt upon her were those of a man impossible to fool.

"He isn't like you!" she flashed. "He wouldn't gallop after a girl and drag her from the saddle of her horse!"

"What a very tame young man he must be." The well-cut lips curled into a mocking smile. "No wonder you don't love him."

"I would sooner be with him than with you . . . you desert barbarian!"

"Would you?" He laughed deep in his throat. "But I have blood in my veins that dilutes the barbarian in me . . . my mother came from Cadiz in Spain, the silver cup as they call it. She had the soft pale skin of a camellia and eyes like marigolds."

Lorna stared at him . . . her heart beat oddly, as if with relief that his mother had been a Latin girl.

"Did your father carry her off and put her in a *harem?*"

She worked as a nurse in a Moroccan hospital." He lifted his cigaret and drew deliberately upon it. "The man I have the honor to call father met her there, and he made her his wife."

"He married her?" Lorna exclaimed.

"He fell deeply in love with her." Suddenly a dangerous little flame burned in the tawny eyes. "A desert love would no doubt alarm a little ice-maiden from the cool shores of Britain?"

"I lived in Paris for a year so I'm not entirely insular."

"And what did you think of Paris? Did you find it fascinating?"

"You speak as if you have been there, *m'sieu.*"

"I was educated there, *mamzelle.*"

Her eyes grew wide, she felt intrigued by the man and at the same time she resented her own stirring of interest. "Really," she said. "Then that explains your knowledge of the French language."

"You speak excellent French yourself, *ma petite blonde.*"

Again there crept into his voice a possessive note, and Lorna drew away from him, back against the cushions, afraid again of this man called Prince Kasim, who lived by desert rules and who took what other men only looked at.

The tent seemed to revolve slowly around Lorna as he rose to his feet and took the *saluki* out of the tent. All was quiet. The large encampment had settled down for the night and the silence was broken only now and again by the yawn of a camel, the jangle of a neck-bell, or the yap of a guard dog. Lorna gave a shiver as a little cold air crept into the tent and stirred the flames in the bowls of the oil-lamps. Shadows stirred across the tapestry walls and the bead curtain moved as if touched by invisible fingers.

Lorna stared at the curtain, and with a sudden sob of torment she jumped to her feet and made as if to flee out of the tent into the night. . . .

Hands caught at her, lean and strong and ruthless. They lifted her and carried her through the bead curtain and there in the amber lamplight he stood holding her and she saw the deep gold of his eyes through his black lashes. Fear of him lent

51

strength to her struggles, but his lithe body was full of a power that made a mockery of her efforts to escape from his arms.

"Little fool, you will wear yourself out." His lips brushed the frightened tears in her blue eyes. "Is there any sense in resistance? You know you cannot get away from me."

"I hate you!" she stormed. "I despise you!"

"I like your spirit." His voice was low-pitched, almost crooning, as if he laughed at her a little. "You are wilful and exciting . . . I believe you would kill me if you could!"

He carried her to the silken bed and she wanted to curl up and die as he put her down on it. He smiled into her eyes, and then he knelt to remove her boots and she felt paralyzed by the fear he aroused in her. Her senses felt drugged. They clamped her to the bed as he tugged off first her right boot, then her left, and tossed them aside. "You don't need a valet for the rest," he said. "I'll turn out the lamps."

She lay biting her knuckles, as if to stop herself screaming, as his tall figure brushed through the curtain and set the beads swinging and dancing. She glanced round wildly and her eyes alighted on a knife that lay beside a bowl of fruit on the bedside table. A richly ornamented *kinzhal* with a slightly curved blade.

Lorna reached for it without hesitation. She was gripping the handle as Prince Kasim came striding back into the *harem* and swift as a little cat she leapt for his heart, grazing him through the linen *kibr* as his hand flashed and caught her by the wrist. He almost snapped her bones as he forced her to drop the *kinzhal*. It fell soundless and glittering to the carpet, and Lorna cried out as the Shaikh bent her backward over his arm. He held her mesmerized while blood from the small wound spread against the white *kibr*.

"Now you have made me rather angry," he said, and his teeth were white against the bronze of his face.

"Please. . . ." Tears of fright made her eyes look like flowers in the rain. "Please don't. . . ."

"I'm not going to beat you," he mocked, and his lips ran like flame to the hollow of her throat. She struggled to escape his lips and suddenly there fell from the pocket of her shirt the flower she had plucked that morning from the wall of the crumbling oasis house. She suffered the Shaikh's bruising clasp as he bent to pick up the flower. The rose-like petals were brushed but they still emitted a faint, brave perfume.

"Why do you carry this flower against your heart?" he demanded.

"Give it to me!" She tried to snatch it from his hand.

"Who gave it to you?" His eyes narrowed and raked her face. "That tame fool who let you ride alone in the desert, where even an Arab is in danger?"

"Yes, it comes from someone I love," she said defiantly. "You can't force me to tell you his name!"

"I thought it was Rodney?"

"Did you?" She snatched the flower, crushed like herself, no longer cool and out of reach of a marauding hand.

"Keep your secrets." He let her go and touched a hand to his breast, as if the knife cut was hurting him a little. He gestured at the bed. "You should sleep comfortably and quite soundly after your day in the desert. Goodnight, my desert captive!"

He swung on his heel, and then paused with a hand on the bead curtain. "I shall be in the other room, all night. And I am always on the alert, even when I sleep."

He was gone, leaving her alone. She could hardly believe that he had gone for the night. Somewhere in the desert a jackal barked, and she gave way to her weariness and sank down across the bed. The flower was pressed to her cheek and a tear slowly watered it as she fell into a deep, exhausted sleep.

CHAPTER FIVE

DAYLIGHT spread through the camp and there was a lot of activity about the coffee fires. The neck-bells of the camels mingled with their grunts as they were pulled to their feet and led off by the camel-boys to graze off the desert shrub. Cloaked figures strode to their horses and a couple of stallions blared at each other until firmly chastised.

These morning sounds penetrated into the big double-tent of the Shaikh, but the girl within did not hear them. She stirred restlessly but did not awake.

Now her lips were relaxed in sleep and her lashes lay still, caught and held by the tears that had dried on her cheeks. Her hair was soft and tousled as a child's, and she had for a while escaped into the dream world of a child again. The camel-bells stole into her dream and became the bells ringing in the convent where men had been excluded; where the gate had opened only to let her into her father's safe keeping.

The early morning activity of the encampment slowly quietened down. The sun was in the tent when Lorna finally aroused from the deep sleep into which she had fallen to find herself beneath the fine netting someone had draped around the bed to keep out the sand flies that appeared when the sun grew warm.

She sat up and pushed aside the netting. She gazed around at surroundings that were at once terribly strange and fearfully familiar.

On the bedside table the cigaret-box lay open, as if earlier a hand had reached for one and forgotten to close the box. A white *kibr* lay discarded across a stool, and Lorna shrank against her pillow as she realized that the Shaikh had entered while she slept; he had drawn the silk coverlet over her and arranged the netting; he had gazed upon her while she was innocently unaware of his eyes. As dreams fled and reality took their place, she gasped as if ice water had been dashed in her face. The events of yesterday and the fact that she was a captive in a Shaikh's tent were as real as the sunshine that blazed outside, inescapable as her own shadow.

She was here in the desert, a reluctant guest of Prince Kasim ben Hassayn, a man of a certain mystery, a man who was as cultured as he was ruthless.

She turned her face into her pillow and tried to blot out his face. It was impossible. The man was so vivid a personality that she could recall his every feature, had forgotten not a word he had said to her during their supper together, and later when he had carried her into this section of the tent. As she remembered her fears of last night she wanted like a child to crawl beneath the bedcovers and hide from the shivering woman that she was.

She stared as the bead curtain moved and Zahra entered the *harem*. Her veil was let down from her face and she was smiling, an indication that the Shaikh was not in residence. She came to the bedside and murmured good morning. She seemed to accept the situation with such composure that Lorna could only suppose that there had been other girls she had waited upon.

Lorna flushed hotly at the thought and could barely answer the girl when she asked if the *lella* had slept well. A finger of sunshine stroked the tousled silk of Lorna's hair, and the Arabian girl looked fascinated, as if never before had she seen someone so fair. The brown eyes slipped to the silken sheet Lorna held against her, and with a tinkle of anklets she ran to a cedarwood chest and took from it a beautiful robe. She brought it to Lorna, who slipped into it without a murmur. It was redolent of a subtle perfume and soft as chiffon to the touch.

"Whose?" Lorna fingered the pure silk. "Tell me!"

The girl looked at Lorna as if she were nice but very perplexing. "A caravan passed us about a week ago, *lella,* from which the Prince Kasim bought garments and perfumes to take with him to the palace for Turqeya."

Turqeya? The exotic name shaped a vision of someone lissome and lovely and raven-haired, and the silk seemed to burn against Lorna's skin.

"The Shaikh gave orders that some of these things were to be brought here for the *lella's* use." Zahra gestured at the cedarwood chest. "Does not the *lella* like such nice things?"

"I would prefer some coffee, and afterward a good hot bath."

"Bath?" Zahra blinked her long dark lashes. "The *lella* took one last night."

"The *lella* will take another this morning!" But as she spoke Lorna remembered that she was in a desert encampment, not a hotel. Water might be scarce here. "I should very much like a bath, if there's sufficient water, Zahra."

"We camp near a well," said the girl, and her expression added that at this rate it would soon run dry. "I will fetch coffee for the *lella,* and I will then heat the water."

"Merci." Lorna smiled at the girl, for she was a pretty thing and about the only friend she had in this place . . . as thoughts of the Shaikh returned, Lorna felt helpless again, and the silk wrap seemed to add to the feeling. He had meant it for a present for another girl until fate had thrown Lorna into his path, and as the events of yesterday swept over her, leading inevitably to her helplessness in his arms last night, a little broken cry escaped her . . .

"Did I alarm the *lella?*" Zahra had returned carrying a tray.

"No . . . I'm all right." How could anyone or anything frighten her as the Shaikh did? Even the thought of his autocratic face made her heart quicken.

Zahra brought the tray to the bed and settled it across her lap. She was longing for a cup of coffee and as she poured it from the copper pot with a long spout, she told Zahra that she need not have brought her anything to eat. "I am not hungry, only very dry. It must be the desert air that makes me feel so thirsty."

"The *lella* is unused to the desert?" Zahra

58

picked up the garment that lay on the stool, and as Lorna watched her the color ebbed and flowed in her cheeks.

"I come from a land where the sun is much cooler and where only on the seashore does one find sand dunes." Lorna spoke with a quiet desperation. England, the convent, and then a year in Paris with her ailing father. How could she have known that her pilgrimage to the East would lead her into a situation she could hardly bear to think about? She, who had scorned men who took liberties, was now deprived of her liberty by a man who didn't care a rap about her feelings!

"The *lella* must eat or the Prince Kasim will be angry with me for not taking proper care of you." Zahra lifted the cover from a dish of crisp rissoles. "Is not the food to the *lella's* liking?"

The spicy aroma of the rissoles rose to Lorna's nostrils and she felt the demands of hunger quite against her will. "It seems that the Shaikh cracks his whip even when he's away from camp," she said as she began to eat.

Zahra gazed at her as if it were an innovation for anyone to speak against him.

"Zahra," Lorna's heart beat very fast, "would you help me to get away?"

The girl backed away from the bed in the same manner as the Shaikh's manservant the evening before. Her lashes veiled her eyes, her entire manner changed from friendliness to something close to hostility. "I go now to fetch the water for the *lella's* bath." She slipped through the bead curtain and Lorna sat staring after her, the little rush of hope turning to ice in her heart.

59

They were all afraid of him! His power was such that no one questioned the presence of an English girl in his tent. Perhaps these people assumed that he did her an honor!

She pushed aside the tray and slipped out of bed; in the alcove where the big copper bowl was kept she found a toilet commode. She glanced about her, noticing again how spotlessly clean everything was kept. The Prince Kasim ben Hussayn was a fastidious man; a small blessing at least. . . .

She paced to and fro across the carpet of the *harem,* her bare feet lost in the tawny leopard skin. She felt caged . . . hurt and betrayed by the desert she had dreamed all her life of visiting.

She sank down on the leopard skin and buried her head against a hassock. Her fair, silky hair fell forward over her face, and the pale gleam of her arms could be seen through the almost transparent robe.

That was how Zahra found her when she returned with the copper kettles of hot water. "Does the *lella* weep?" The girl touched her hair and Lorna turned a tearless face to her and gazed upward with clouded blue eyes.

"You think I should be smiling?" she asked.

"The Shaikh is much of a man and very handsome." Zahra's puzzlement was that of an Arabian girl who had been reared to the idea that men were superior beings. She was unaware that girls like Lorna were not handed over to a stranger and subjected to his will without a murmur of protest.

"The Shaikh Kasim is the cruellest person I

60

have ever met," Lorna said bitterly. "I wish that he be made to suffer, and I wish it with all my heart."

Zahra's great brown eyes were fixed in horror upon Lorna. "The Sidi Kasim is not cruel to his people . . . !

"I have seen him whip a man," Lorna said with a shudder.

"The man must have deserved his punishment, and the *lella* must understand that here in the desert our laws are different from those in a city."

"I think the desert makes people cruel," Lorna whispered.

Zahra shrugged, as if the English girl's idea of cruelty was not hers. She filled the copper bowl with steaming water and added the scented oil that made the water soft and foamy. From a low table beside the bowl that served as a bath she took a large sponge and gazed silently at Lorna.

"I can manage on my own," Lorna assured her.

"I will wash the *lella* and make her skin glow as they do in the *hamman*. It is a good feeling . . . relaxing."

"No. . . ." Lorna was slightly shocked. "I prefer to wash myself."

The *lella* should not be shy." Zahra spoke now as if to an infant. "There is no need for shame when the body is without flaw."

A sensible point of view, Lorna had to admit, but her cheeks were pink as she undressed and stepped into the scented water.

Zahra sponged her from head to foot, and there was a roughness to the sponge that made her tingle and feel beautifully fresh. Zahra did not meet her eyes, however, when she winced at the touch of the

61

sponge against a bruise on her upper right arm. It was dark against her white skin, a mark of the Shaikh's anger just after she had tried to stab him. She touched the bruise with her fingertip and it pleased her that she had left her mark on him. The *kinzhal* had cut him and there would be a small scar.

Bathed and wrapped in a towel she stood looking at her breeches and shirt. The breeches could be brushed, the boots polished, but the shirt needed washing.

"She knelt by the cedarwood chest and examined its contents. There was among the silks and velvets a sleeveless tunic of blue brocade that could serve as a blouse if tucked into her breeches . . . she was darned if she would wear the silk trousers that went with it.

Zahra tried in vain to persuade her to wear the full outfit. "I am not a *harem* girl," Lorna said cuttingly. "I won't wear see-through pants and that is final!"

"If you anger the Prince Kasim, then he will be unkind." Zahra lowered her lashes. "Men are that way."

"You mean they like their own way." Lorna stamped into her boots and zippered the waistband of her breeches. The tunic made a passable blouse and the material was quite beautiful with its shimmering mixture of blues. You are very young, Zahra, to know about men and their demanding ways."

"I am married," Zahra said shyly. "My husband Yusuf is in charge of one of the horse stockades, a very important position, for the Sidi Kasim has a great love of horses and his are the finest for many miles of desert land."

Lorna gazed at the girl in some astonishment. She seemed to be surely no more than seventeen years old and yet already she bore the burden of a household and was subject to the will of a husband. "Now I understand why you were veiled last night," she said. "An Arabian doesn't like his wife to show her face to another man, and you are extremely pretty."

Zahra blushed, the tinge of pink beneath the pale gold of her skin making her prettier still. "Yusuf is kind to me," she said.

"So he ought to be! He's lucky to have you."

Lorna swung to the mirror to brush her hair, and the look she gave her reflection was a wry one. The sleeveless tunic glistened against her pale skin, and with her fair hair brushed smooth she had the look of a good-looking page at some barbaric court. As she laid down the brush her fingers encountered the *agal* the Shaikh had left lying on the dresser. She recoiled from it as from a snake. For a few minutes she had mercifully forgotten him, now she had to escape from the *harem*, if only into the outer tent.

She stood at the bead curtain, gripping it. "You must not empty that great bowl of water on your own," she said to Zahra, who was tidying up after her. "I will send Hassan to help you."

"The *lella* is kind," Zahra said with her warm, soft smile.

"The *lella* is a fool!" The words came wrenched from Lorna. "A wilful and obstinate little donkey, Zahra, who should have listened to a friend who warned me to beware of the desert and the dangers it holds."

The bead curtain clattered into place behind her, and once again she found herself in the main section of the spacious tent. The flap was pinned back and the sunlight streamed in, cloaking the white-robed Hassan as he appeared and gave her a polite *salaam*.

Lorna stared at the tent opening. It seemed to offer a means of escape and in her desperation she felt she would have walked into the desert to get away from Kasim ben Hussayn.

She told Hassan to go and help Zahra to dispose of the bath water, and with an inscrutable countenance he obeyed the order. Lorna walked out into the sunshine and glanced about her with desperately eager eyes. They encountered those of a man who lounged against a mound of riding saddles. He had the lean face of a hawk, and as Lorna walked away from the Shaikh's tent, along a pathway that led into the main area of the encampment, the Arab followed her. She threw him a look over her shoulder and again his eyes were as hooded as a hawk's as he easily kept pace with her hurrying figure.

She paused near a camp fire, on the edge of which stood a row of long-spouted, fire-darkened coffee pots. "I suppose you have been told to be my shadow," she said in French.

The Arab bowed his head slightly, his nose and his cheekbones jutting hard against his dark, sunburned skin. His robes were startlingly white against his swarthiness, and it struck Lorna that he was far more Arabian-looking than the Shaikh.

"I won't be followed about as if I'm a prisoner!" she said desperately.

"I have my orders, *madame.*" His French was rather harsh.

"Sans doute," she rejoined. "His Highness is fond of giving orders!"

"Madame may take a walk and she may look about the camp."

"May I also take a ride on one of the master's horses?"

"I fear not, *madame,* not until the Sidi Kasim gives his permission."

Lorna bit her lip and hatred of the Sidi Kasim raged in her. She walked on, her fair head held high, aware of the glances that were cast at her by the people about the camp. Children peeped at her from around the long indigo-blue skirts of their mothers, and she noticed how the low black tents were pitched to face the east, and that their hangings were removed in daylight so that they looked like cool pavilions.

She saw gazelle hounds sprawled in patches of shade, and the stockades in which young horses were roaming about. They had a sleek, tempered look of speed and Lorna ached to get her hands on one of them. How swiftly she could then ride away from the man who held her captive in his desert encampment!

As if reading her thoughts her young Arab guide directed her toward the green shade of the palm trees that guarded the well of the oasis. Date palms from which hung great bunches of red-golden fruit. Lorna walked beneath the rustling palms and remembered that only the day before she had been free as a bird. She had not dreamed that the Oasis of Fadna would prove a place of bad omen.

Fadna . . . Fate. She might have guessed, but had been blinded by the happiness her father had found there; the inspiration and a certain peace.

"Please lead the way back," she said to her guide, and there was an urgency in her voice which he evidently mistook for an eagerness to be again in the tent of the Shaikh. A smile touched his lips as he touched a lean hand to his forehead and his eyes, as if to say that his thoughts were hers, his eyes at her command.

Back in the great tent she threw herself down on the smaller divan and stared at each object, each item of furniture in turn. The lamps were beautifully wrought, the carpets glowed with color, the ornaments of copper and brass were valuable.

Cushions, carpets, and rich hangings were purely antique, but there was also a small cabinet of books, and a writing desk in a secluded corner of the tent. It was inlaid with mother-of-pearl and a nest of many small drawers caught and held her gaze.

She arose after a moment's hesitation and approached the desk. She traced with her fingertip the gilded lettering on the front of a leather writing case, and then she tried the drawers and found them locked . . . all but one.

She pulled it open and peered into the tiny aperture. Some objects glittered there and she took them out, breathing with suppressed excitement as she saw that she held a locket on a chain, and an ivory crucifix attached to a rosary of many tiny beads. Lorna opened the locket and found inside the miniature of a young woman with Madonna-styled hair and a pair of wonderful, faintly slanting eyes.

"My mother was from Spain," her captor had said.

His mother, this lovely creature with the warmly curved mouth . . . a woman who had entered of her own free will into the enclosed life of the *harem*. The woman who must have delighted in her son as a child, but who might not have lived to see him grow into so ruthless and handsome a man.

Lorna closed the locket and returned it with the crucifix to the tiny drawer. Her hands plunged into the pockets of her breeches. The very fact that her captor was a man of breeding and education made worse the infamy of his abduction of her. She gazed out hopelessly through the opening of the tent . . . out there were people but none of them would help her to escape.

In one hour, in two, he would return. He would come striding into the tent, and Lorna could picture in detail his strong, sun-bitten features; his tallness and his masculine grace. She shrank from meeting again the eyes that were as tawny as a leopard's. The strength seemed to leave her limbs and she sank down on the divan and buried her face desperately in the cushions.

"Let his horse throw him and break his neck!" she whispered imploringly.

CHAPTER SIX

IT was the jangling of camel-bells that aroused the camp out of the spell laid upon it by the afternoon heat.

Lorna had fallen asleep among the cushions of the divan, but now she awoke and sat up ruffling her hair. The tent had grown dim and she realized that the day had almost waned. She arose from the divan and walked to the doorway to watch the sunset.

Women in long robes were busy about the camp fires, and men on horseback had appeared, adding to the sudden vivacity of the scene. A small boy ran to be scooped up in his father's arms and the murmur of deep voices mingled with the jingling of harness as the red and gold sunset flared over the Prince's camp.

Lorna stood half-hidden in the tent doorway and watched the scene with wondering eyes. Smoke arose from the brushwood fires and mingled its scent with the aroma of coffee and the spicy tang of stew cooking in the pots that hung over the flames. Someone strummed a stringed instrument and the music was strange and haunting.

At any other time Lorna would have been enchanted to be a guest in a colorful camp in the desert, but with the going down of the sun she felt a chill in the air . . . soon now the Shaikh would return. She tried not to think of this as she listened to the chatter of the women as they carried water jars from the well. They were graceful as they walked to their tents, their anklets making a soft music.

The last rays of evening shone in the west, an almost tortured burst of color . . . the passion stored up in nature, the cruelty, the beauty, and the sadness.

> *"As if the sunset when the day did swoon,*
> *Had drawn some wild confession from the*
> *moon."*

The sun died, leaving little quivers of scarlet in the sky, expressive of pain. Night fell almost at once and a star burned over the camp.

It was then that Lorna noticed the trio of horsemen riding in from the desert, cloaked, seated on high-stepping mounts whose harness shone silver as they cantered into the firelight.

A hand of ice seemed to grip Lorna's heart. For seconds on end she couldn't move, her gaze was fixed upon the foremost rider as he wheeled his black mount and dismounted with a wide flaring of his riding cloak. A commanding figure, taller than those about him, reaching out a hand to fondle the horse that had carried him well throughout the day. The stallion neighed softly and thrust its head against the broad shoulder.

Where did he go? What did he do during the long hours he was away from the encampment?

The answer came all too clearly to Lorna as her gaze dwelt on the tall figure and she heard him giving orders in his deep voice. He was in control of outlying villages and hillside communities. He went to supervise them, to attend the council meetings, to sit in judgment on law breakers.

His own self-made laws were not to be judged!

Lorna withdrew into the tent, and a moment later. Hassan came to light the lamps. As they bloomed and cast their saffron glow, the pallor of Lorna's face was revealed. Her eyes were dark blue with apprehension and her heart beat fast. It was pride alone that saved her from fleeing into the inner tent. She wouldn't give him the satisfaction of seeing her cowed and frightened.

"I will bring a jug of freshly made limoon," said Hassan in his quiet way. "The master is fond of it."

Lorna looked at the manservant and barely restrained herself from saying that the master's likes and dislikes were of less interest to her than the moths that flew in from the darkness to flutter about the lamps. "No doubt he will be thirsty," she said, with a cool composure that belied her inner tension.

Hassan bowed and withdrew, leaving her alone in the lamplit tent. She thrust her hands into the pockets of her breeches and every fibre of her body was taut; she hardly breathed, hardly moved, a pale statue in the center of the carpet. There came the jingle of spurs and a cold thrill ran through her as with his soundless stride he entered the tent. His cloak was swept back over his shoulder, the silk lining a flash of scarlet against his white tunic and breeches. His supple knee-boots matched the lining color. He was a barbaric figure as he stood just inside the entrance and swept his eyes over her.

"I am sorry to be so late," he said in the deep voice that seemed to vibrate along her nerves. "I hope you have not been too impatient for my tardy return, *ma fille.*"

She bravely met his startling eyes, tawny as the desert sands. "I hoped your horse had thrown you and broken your neck!" she flung at him.

"A woman in a temper is one who has been lonely," he mocked.

"Did you hope to find me in tears, Prince Kasim?"

He smiled wickedly as he flung aside his whip with its long plaited lash . . . the weapon he was so adroit at using. "You have too much spirit to be the weeping kind, *ma fille.*"

"How disappointing for you, *m'sieu.*"

He unbuckled his cloak and dropped it across a divan. "On the contrary," his eyes flicked the blue tunic that revealed the slender bareness of her arms, "it intrigues me that tonight, or tomorrow, you may try again to plunge a knife into me."

"The blade would break," she said scornfully, but even as she spoke her gaze dwelt on the broad chest she had nicked with the gemmed knife. "You have a heart of stone!"

"My heart of stone is not unmoved by the look of you, *chérie.*" His glance lingered on her hair, which the lamplight haloed about her pale heart of a face. "I wondered all day if I had imagined your sun-colored hair, your eyes deep blue as jasmine, your mouth that pleads so eloquently . . . !"

There he broke off as Hassan entered the tent

71

with a jug of limoon and stemmed glasses. He placed the tray on one of the low tables and asked his master at what time he would like dinner.

"In one hour, Hassan. I have a fancy for roast lamb, and to follow, those small sultana pancakes."

"The lamb is on the spit, *sidi."* The manservant smiled. "I know your appetite when your ride has been a long one. Water is also heating for my lord's steam bath when he is ready."

The tent flap fell into place behind the Shaikh's servant, and Lorna felt amazement at the lordly way he lived here in camp. Even a steam bath was provided for his pleasure . . . the pleasure he obviously took in being utterly clean.

"Please pour me a glass of limoon," he said casually.

"Your servant has just left," she retorted, hands clenched in her pockets.

"Pour it, *chérie."* A soft, dangerous note came into his voice, and seething inwardly she went to the table and filled a glass with the cool lime juice.

"Now bring it to me," he ordered.

"Yes, my lord." She turned from the table, walked straight up to him and flung the contents of the glass full in his arrogant face. Then, white-faced, she watched as the drops ran down on to his *kibr* and a flame leaped alight in his eyes.

"Now do you feel better?" he asked.

"Much better," she rejoined. "I only wish it had been acid . . . I'd like to spoil for ever your devil's face!"

"You have the temper of a little devil yourself." He took a handkerchief from his pocket and wiped his face, and then he took a swift step forward and before she could evade his touch she was caught and held against him; each curve and line of her was crushed to his hard body.

"How much you hate me, eh?" His lips were tormentingly close to her own, his eyes sparkled dangerously. "First you try to stab me, now you try to arouse my temper in the hope that I will break your neck. It is too lovely a neck to break, *ma chère*. I would much sooner kiss it."

As she felt his lips, she closed her eyes and blotted out his face, but she couldn't numb her senses and not feel his urgent mouth against her throat, the delicate line of her cheek, her temple. She shuddered from head to foot as his mouth closed warm and hard on hers, forcing back her head until she was utterly consumed by his passionate kiss.

"Please . . . let me go," she pleaded, when at last she could speak.

"There." He released her from his arms with a soft laugh. "You are free."

"Don't torment me!" Her eyes blazed jewel-blue and beseeching in the tumbled frame of her soft hair. "Give me a horse and a guide . . . let me return to Yraa. I'll say nothing about being here!"

"You would spare me punishment for my sins?" he taunted, pouring a second glass of limoon and drinking it down thirstily. "You would say nothing because you would hate anyone to know that in the desert you have met your match. How many men, my little fury, have you put to flight with your scorn and your coldness?"

"You brute!" Color flamed into her cheeks. "That horse thief was less outrageous than you,

73

with your steam bath, your books, and your Spanish mother!"

"We will not discuss my mother," he said curtly. "She at least had a warm heart."

"If I am so cold, then I am surely out of place in the tent of a prince? Surely you would prefer someone a little more ardent?"

"One of my *filles de joie?*" He quirked a black eyebrow. "As you know, I breed horses and have a great fondness for them. Now and again one turns out to have a wilful streak and I enjoy the taming process."

"You mean you enjoy breaking its spirit," she retorted.

"Only one of my horses has ever come close to being broken in spirit, and I flogged in front of you the man responsible."

"I take it the abduction of a *girl* troubles you hardly at all? I am aware, Prince Kasim, that in your opinion a female can hardly hope to compete with the attractions of a good horse, but as it happens I am not an Arabian girl and I resent being held a prisoner to your whims. I have rights and you can't altogether ignore them. I am not a *thing.*"

"No Arabian girl was ever as lucid," he said. "You think the authorities will start combing the desert for you, eh? They will no doubt take a look around the Oasis of Fadna, they will make a few inquiries and upon learning that you are headstrong, wilful, and most unusually beautiful, they will shrug fatalistically and say you were more than foolish to go riding alone."

Lorna gazed at him, speechlessly. "You . . . you have no intention of letting me return to the

74

Ras Jusuf?" A terrible weakness seemed to sweep over her and she wanted to give way to it, to crumple to the carpet, to weep and claw like a little chained animal. "You mean to keep me here?"

"For as long as it pleases me," he said lazily. "A man looks forward to some distraction after the affairs of the day, and you are very distracting, *ma fille*. You have spirit, and I like that. You are lovely but cool, and I find that a challenge."

"You have no mercy," she flung at him.

"You, as yet, have no awareness of the body and its merciless demands," he rejoined.

She stared at him, her every nerve shocked and tingling. "You are a devil!" she choked.

"Perhaps—but then a woman's face is the devil's mirror when it's blue-eyed, soft-lipped, tantalizing."

He drew open the flap of the tent and as he stood there, looking at her, his leopard grace and assurance were an affront. His possessive glance outraged her.

"Garments were provided so that I might see you looking like a girl instead of a charming boy. You will wear them!"

"Things you bought to please a slave girl at your palace?" Her lip curled. "You will have to force me into them!"

"I am sure I would get more pleasure out of the procedure than you would, *ma fille*." His eyes were wickedly amused. "Turqeya is my sister, not a slave."

With a sardonic bow he was gone, leaving his forceful image superimposed upon the closed flap. Lorna heard him address someone outside, and she lifted a hand to her throat as if to still her frantic pulse. He spoke to one of his Arab guards, installed at the entrance of the tent to ensure that she did not run away. . . .

Until he tired of her! Until then she would be kept in this silken trap with its lamplit shadows. She would be forced to endure the Prince's company . . . and his caresses.

She fled from the thought into the *harem,* and there in a while Zahra came to help her dress. Lorna was quiet and subdued. She made no protest about wearing a smoky velvet tunic with tiny pearl buttons from throat to waist, or the silken trousers caught in at the ankle. She stepped into the *babouches* of ruby red with upturned toes, and allowed Zahra to brush her hair until it shone more silkily than her garments.

So Turqeya was the Shaikh's sister. He bought her gifts, so he must be fond of her. Lorna tried to imagine so ruthless a man being fond of anyone. Fondness, affection indicated the presence of a heart, and to Lorna the man was quite heartless.

"Zahra?"

"Yes, *lella?*"

"Is the master's sister very pretty?"

"The Princess Turqeya is like a golden doll, with lashes in which a moth might become entangled, and dusky hair to her waist. It is said that many wealthy men have asked to marry her, but the Prince Kasim has refused all of them on her behalf."

"Does her father have no say in the matter?"

"The Emir is too busy a man to concern himself with a mere daughter. The Sidi Kasim is the Emir's

76

great pride and joy. He has let him have always whatever he has desired."

"I can well believe that!" Lorna bit her lip. Even with Zahra she was ashamed of revealing the anguish and the fear that she felt, and she turned away from the mirror, scornful of her *harem* image.

"The *lella* is not pleased with her appearance?" Zahra asked anxiously. "Perhaps if you had ornaments to wear about your throat and gems for your ears—"

"Don't!" Lorna gave a laugh that held a hint of tears. "I look enough like an odalisque without adding to the picture. I look as though I am going to a carnival!"

"What is this—carnival?" Zahra was very perplexed by this fair-haired *roumia* who occupied the forbidden tent of a most powerful Prince and yet was not pleased or proud.

"A carnival is a parade of people, Zahra, who can only be brave or gay behind a mask. It's like life, really. We smile to hide a pain. We laugh to hold back the tears!"

"Everything is *mektub*," Zahra said in all seriousness. "We cannot help the things we do. It is written!"

"Which is like saying, Hate the sin but love the sinner. He sins to written orders."

Lorna gripped the bead curtain and steeled herself to enter the outer tent. Hassan was there laying the table. The Shaikh had not yet returned and she felt his manservant following her with his eyes as she went outside to breathe the cool night air and to look at the stars. A shadow moved in the shadows around the great tent, and Lorna knew it

77

was her guard, silently watching her as she stood in the silvery darkness and breathed the strange scents of the encampment mingling with those that stole in from the desert beyond the oasis.

She had a longing to see the vast and silent desert beneath the climbing moon, but with a sigh she returned to the tent. Zahra and Hassan had departed. The saffron glow of the lamps added to the luxury of the mellow carpets, the sheen of the cushions and the hangings and the copper ornaments. On the knee-high table in front of the large divan stood a round dish with a pewter dome covering it. There was wine to accompany the meal, and Lorna as she gazed about her was struck anew by the realization that her captor was so oddly cosmopolitan.

Lorna tensed as he entered the tent, bare-headed, fresh from his steam bath, and clad in a *kibr* which was deeply open at his brown throat. His presence overwhelmed Lorna. He was like some vital and dangerous animal whose purr was uncertain.

His thonged sandals made no sound on the carpets as he came to her. He took her hands and at the softening of his gaze she grew even more afraid of him. "Fortune made you very fair," he said, and he brushed his lips across her fingertips. "Smile at me," he coaxed.

She was frozen. She stood like a statue, inanimate but for the pounding of her heart at his nearness and his touch.

"Can you smile?"

"Smiling is for happy people," she said.

"Does it not make you happy, my Dinarzade, to

78

be told that you are beautiful?" His own smile slashed a deep line in his sun-bronzed cheek. "Dinarzade was the girl who knew nothing about love, by the way. She was very innocent."

"Surely you would prefer a Scheherazade?" Lorna tilted her chin. "Or have you become bored with all those you have known?"

He merely laughed at her, his teeth flashing white in arrogant amusement. "Come, let us eat! I have been riding hard all day and I groan for food."

They went to the divan, where the Shaikh sprawled with the grace of a leopard and uncovered the spit-roasted lamb which gave off a delectable aroma of herbs. A knife and fork were laid ready for Lorna's use, and now and again her companion glanced at her as if amused by her demure way of eating.

"I have lived more in the desert than elsewhere," he said. "The ways of the tribesmen are mine in most ways, though I drink wine."

"It amazes me that you don't spill rice and peas all over you," she said, taking a sip at her own glass of French wine.

"It is a knack to eat this way—shall I show you?"

"No." She shook her head and avoided his glance. She was intensely aware of his maleness, the width of his shoulders, the strong column of his throat merging into his deep chest. His skin in the lamplight had a bronze look. His eyes were slumbrous between the dense lashes.

"Of what are you thinking, *ma fleur?*" He said it casually as he dipped his fingers into a small bowl of water and wiped them on a hand towel.

A shiver ran all the way through her. "My flower. . . ." That he should say it, like a lover, shocked her to the core.

"Am I not entitled to thoughts of my own?" she fenced.

"You are welcome to your thoughts . . . though half the time I can read them." His glance played over her, and then with a smile he folded a pancake and bit into it with careless enjoyment. "Come, join me. These are excellent."

"I've had enough." She dipped her fingers in the little bowl and dried them. "I . . . I haven't been out riding like you to work up an appetite. Even when I took a small walk, one of your men shadowed me every inch of the way."

"Would you like to ride?"

She looked at him with an unbelieving eagerness. "May I? Will you let me?"

"Will I let you?" He leaned forward and held her with his eyes, golden in the lamplight. "I may let you do many things, *chérie,* but I won't let you go."

"I . . . I should so like to ride." Her eyes were huge and wistful.

"Then you shall ride," he said, and he smiled at her as she sat among the cushions of the shared divan, his toy, his whim, to be indulged or ignored as the mood took him.

CHAPTER SEVEN

"There is a splendid savagery about my land and you should see it," he went on. "You will ride with me, and when I am away from camp you will ride with one of my men. You have learned already that it is dangerous for you to ride alone . . . I could not permit that."

"You know I'd ride off!" She resented his nearness and his power over her. "If ever I get the chance I shall walk off, and I don't care if I die in the desert."

"What a dramatic threat." He ran a finger down her cheek. "You would suffer the torments of heat and thirst and loneliness to get away from me, eh? We are many miles from Yraa."

"Won't you consider my . . . family?" she said desperately. "Would you like to see your own sister in my . . . predicament?"

"Turqeya would not be foolish enough to ride alone in the desert. She has the wisdom of the East in her blood."

"Perhaps Turqeya is wise because she judges all men by her brother!" Lorna met his eyes bravely. "Perhaps I have been unwise because I judged all men by my father. He was gallant and kind."

"You speak in the past tense!"

Lorna's hand crushed a cushion . . . she had let slip the fact that her father was dead and could not be concerned for her. "Don't you care that I hate you?" she cried.

"I should care if you were indifferent to me." He unclenched her fingers from the cushion and held her hand so that it was very small and white in his brown hand. "Hate is an intriguing emotion. I prefer it to the cloying pretence of love for the sake of gifts and favors. There are women, little one, who think only of themselves."

"I am sure you are an expert at judging them!" She wanted to snatch her hand from his, but knew it would be futile to try.

"I would not presume to call myself an expert." The smile deepened in his eyes as he rang the little brass bell that stood on the table. Almost at once Hassan appeared with their French coffee in its long-spouted pot, with the cups in silver holders.

"*Madame* will pour the coffee," the Shaikh said to him.

Hassan bowed and withdrew, and Lorna cast a look at the man beside her, passionate with resentment. She took hold of the pot of steaming coffee and he lounged beside her without moving, his eyes upon her face, daring her silently to do with the coffee what she had done with the limoon.

Lorna bent her fair head and poured the coffee into the cups. It was dark, aromatic, and with a set face she handed him his cup.

"Do you like our desert cuisine?" he asked her.

"It's quite surprising."

To drink coffee with him among the cushions of the divan was a disturbing intimacy. Night had fallen like a dark over the encampment, muffling the sounds from outside the tent. Moths clustered around the lamps, drawn to the flames to find a painful ecstasy.

Lorna finished her coffee and rose nervously to her feet. She wandered about the tent, touching ornaments, feeling and seeing nothing but the lounging figure of the Prince. Her nerves tightened when he leaned forward casually to take and light a cigaret.

"Won't you join me?" he said. "A cigaret will help to steady your nerves."

"My nerves are fine, thank you." She went to the doorway of the tent and held open the flap, wishing she could escape from the intimate atmosphere if only for a short while.

She tensed as the Prince came and stood behind her. "You are restless," he said. "Would you like to take a walk to the edge of the oasis?"

"Oh. . . more than anything!" She went to slip outside and he held her back a moment.

"The night air is cold. You must wear my cloak." He fetched it from across the tent and clasped it about her. "You will have to drape some of it over your arm—there, now you are a charming boy again."

They went outside, where tribesmen sat cloaked around their coffee fires, listening to the music of a stringed instrument, a soft wailing in the night that blended with the mysterious shapes of tents and camels, their long necks stretched along the sand as they slept.

The men inclined their heads as the couple passed by, but they did not look openly at the slim, cloaked figure of Lorna. This was their way of being polite to their master's guest.

The strange music died away behind Lorna and her escort. The palm trees stood tall and faintly rustling in the oasis, and when they came to the moonlit sands it was like walking through milk. Silvery-violet shadows lay in the laps of the dunes. Each star above was like a small golden flame, and the air that Lorna breathed was wild and cool.

Shadow and mystery, an infinity of space that quietened her nerves and made her almost grateful to Prince Kasim for allowing her to witness the magic of the desert by moonlight.

"The desert is like a woman," he murmured. "Seductive and challenging, with depths in which a man might get lost forever. I have known it in all moods, yet each day its sweeping spaces offer something new. A fresh challenge, a certain torment, and then at night its cool caress, or its crescent moon—the claw of the lover."

The wind whispered across the illimitable spaces, and Lorna glanced at the man beside her and saw his profile moulded firm against the glow of the moon. He was a part of all this, as the falcons were, and the golden sand cats who lurked among the sandstone rocks.

"Do you hear the call of the desert?" His eyes flashed to meet hers and she saw how they glinted in the moonlight.

"I am fascinated," she admitted. "But I am also frightened by the vastness, the sense of its eternity while we are so mortal."

"Yes," he smiled, "already the desert has touched you. We must ride *l'aube* you and I. When you have been in the desert at dawn, you will then be completely captivated."

"Is not my captivation already an accomplished fact, *m'sieu?*" She drew his cloak around her as the wind touched her throat and ruffled her hair.

He gazed down at her, at her silvered hair and her pale heart-shaped face in which the blue-violet eyes were set like flowers. He reached for her and her fingertips pressed against his chest as he gathered her close to him. *"Le desert de l'amour,"* he softly mocked, as she struggled with him and was defeated by his strength. "Come, you know there is a devil in me, *chérie*. Rouse him at your peril."

"When will you let me go?" she implored.

"Don't talk of going when it is but a night and a day since I brought you here." As he spoke he took her lips. He seemed to want to crush her, to be cruel and caressing at the same time.

"Theldja—snow—I should let the desert have you and be rid of such a flake of ice," he murmured against her mouth.

"Better the desert than you!" She fought to turn her head away, but he caught her by the chin and made her submit to his demanding gaze there in the desert moonlight. Across the sweeping hillocks of sand came the howl of a jackal as it hunted its prey.

"You look at me with the eyes of a trapped gazelle." He bent his head and closed her eyes with kisses, and then he lifted her in his arms and carried her beneath the palm trees, past the tents and the smoking fires, across the compound that separated his tent from all the rest.

His arms were strong and possessive around her

as he carried her inside. But again that night he left her alone in the *harem*.

Time in the desert had an endless quality. It passed without the ticking of clocks, or the many signs and signals of city life. The men of the desert told the time by the sun, and their life was unhurried but continually active.

In the beginning Lorna had counted the days, but soon she ceased to do so and lost track, almost, of how long she had been at the desert camp. It was an immense one, and Lorna soon learned that the Shaikh's control over his people was absolute; a leadership based on firmness of character, magnetic personality, and an untiring interest in their rugged way of life.

Sometimes there were family quarrels and he swiftly intervened before a feud could develop. Upon one occasion a tribesman came to ask the master's advice about his daughter, who was disobedient and flighty. The Shaikh interviewed the girl and promptly found for her a young and good-looking husband.

Lorna was astounded. "He's almost a stranger to her," she protested.

"She needs a husband," he said calmly. "Soon she will forget her foolishness and be a model wife."

"What a despot you are!" Lorna flicked her palmetto fan at a hovering wasp. "You seem to regard women as creatures without minds or hearts of their own."

"A woman has to be handled as one handles a spirited filly, so that she feels the tension of the rein and won't lose her head." He lounged on the divan

86

and stretched a booted leg; his cigaret smoke half-veiled the expression in his eyes.

"Apart from the rein there is the whip," Lorna murmured.

She felt the flick of tawny eyes. "Have these weeks as my guest taught you so little?" he asked. "A real woman likes to feel that she is mastered. She enjoys her fear of the man who is unafraid of her. Women are mysterious creatures, *ma fille,* and there are men who go in awe of your sex. I am sure you must have known some of these namby-pamby boys to have become so haughty."

"Haughty—me?" she exclaimed. "You have room to talk! You lord it over hundreds of tribesmen, run their lives for them, rush girls into marriage with men they hardly know, and accuse me of pride!"

"I should like you less if you were not proud." His eyes smiled through a gust of cigaret smoke. "You must admit that in my handling of such a high-strung filly as yourself, I never break your spirit or your pride."

Lorna turned away from him and gazed from the doorway of the tent at the activity about the camp, always more in evidence when the Shaikh was in residence. Filly indeed! He had his nerve . . . more nerve and gall than any other man alive!

Her fingers clenched on the pinned-back flap of the tent as she thought of the things she had learned about him during these enforced weeks in the desert. He was utterly fearless, and strangely gentle with small children and all animals. His temper when roused was a frightening one, and now and again he lost it with a disobedient follower. He

confused her as no one else had ever done . . .
sometimes she almost admired him, and was
intrigued by his many Latin ways.

Absorbed in her thoughts she didn't hear him
cross the tent, but suddenly his arm was locked
about her slender waist. "Do you still find me
hateful?" he murmured, his warm breath against
her temple.

"Surely you have no need to ask?" When he
held her there was no getting away from him, but
she could still fight him with words. She could still
let him know that his touch was hateful to her.

"What would you have me do?" He laughed and
kissed the nape of her neck. "Pile my sins on the
back of a goat and send it into the desert to atone
for me?"

"You would need more than one goat," she
retorted.

He laughed and swung her to face him and she
saw the admiration gleaming in his eyes as they
swept her hair, her face, her mouth that was a curve
of soft scarlet against her sun-honeyed skin. "Sticks
and stones, but never words," he mocked. "Words I
can silence with a kiss."

Holding her in the circle of his arm he bent over
her and put his threat into action. His kiss was
smoky from his cigaret, his nearness was like a
flame through her body, his arm felt like steel about
her.

"I intend to visit the encampment of a friend
tomorrow," he said. "You may ride part of the way
with me, but Ahmed will escort you back to camp.
Come, your promise that you will behave yourself
while I am away."

"Ahmed is too keen a watchdog to be fooled by any of my tricks," she rejoined. "He fears too much the displeasure of his Shaikh to give me the pleasure of escaping him."

"My men are certainly aware that I would be— annoyed." Kasim released her and strode to his desk. He switched on the lamp and sat down to write in the big ledger that was bound in leather and unreadable as far as Lorna was concerned. She watched, fascinated, as his pen inscribed the beautiful script that made each page in the ledger a work of art. He was also clever at sketching his sleek Arabian horses, but she would not permit herself to dislike him any the less for having something in common with the father she had dearly loved and lost.

She never talked of her father to her captor. She refused stubbornly to share with him the memories that were so precious and painful to her.

When in a while he glanced up, she looked away from him and went to the bookcase, from which she took a copy of *The Silver Cup,* a history of Cadiz, where his mother had been born and where she had spent her girlhood. Her signature was in the book. Her name had been Elena.

Lorna curled down on a rug and tried to lose herself in the book, but all the time, with her every nerve, she was aware of the Shaikh. From the corner of her eye she watched the smoke curling from his cigaret; she saw the outline of his muscles beneath the silk *kibr.*

When would he let her go?

She feared to ask him . . . she feared his answer. She had learned that in lots of ways the life

89

of a powerful Prince was a solitary one. He could not completely unbend with his people and risk his authority. In the privacy of his tent he could relax and toss aside his cares and duties, and though at times he treated Lorna with indifference, he seemed to get pleasure out of their conversations and their rides.

Then as if reading her thoughts, he said sardonically: "You should count yourself fortunate that you are not in the *harem* of a conventional Shaikh, with four wives and a batch of concubines."

"Conventional?" she exclaimed.

"Yes. I am the unconventional one, *ma fille.* I have but you in my *harem,* much to the astonishment of my men."

"That's here in camp," she said, a flame on each cheekbone. "What of your *harem* in the palace?"

"Empty, alas."

"Do you grow tired of your women, so quickly?"

"If you are asking in a subtle way if I grow tired of you, then the answer is no." His teeth glimmered in a smile. "Just think how much less of my company you would have if you shared me with a *harem* of Eastern beauties."

"I'm surprised you haven't a large *harem,*" she said, as casually as she could, her eyes averted from his wide shoulders, his striking profile, his black hair that gleamed in the lamplight with little hints of blue.

"I am away in the desert so much of the time that it would be unfair of me to collect women only to neglect them," he drawled.

"You flatter yourself they would miss you!"

"Once a woman has enjoyed the companionship of a man, she misses him when he leaves her."

"I should welcome the day!"

He laughed lazily. "I should miss the barbs on your tongue, my girl." He bent his head and resumed his work on the ledgers, leaving Lorna free to study him. From the black point of hair stabbing the nape of his neck, to the riding boots he still wore, he was a fine looking man and there were facets to his personality that she liked despite herself. She wondered if he rejected some of the customs of the desert out of deference to the memory of his Spanish mother?

As Lorna sat pondering the complex nature of her captor, there came the sound of a voice outside the tent. "See who wants me, Lorna." He always shook her when he spoke English, and her hand trembled slightly as she opened the flap and found herself confronted by Ahmed. Upon seeing his master at the desk, he broke into voluble speech. At once Kasim rose from his writing and there was an eager glint in his eyes.

"Come!" he caught at Lorna's hand. "The Kaid whom I visit tomorrow has sent me a gift. Let us go and take a look!"

His followers had grown used to Lorna by now and she went among them without any of her former shyness. Several of the women greeted her and children ran to take sweets from the pocket of her breeches. She smiled and spoke to them, startlingly fair and fragile among the throne of sun-dark desert dwellers.

The chattering crowd gave passage to the Shaikh, and to the *lella* who was so often with him, and there in the open space in the center of the camp a couple of men held the halter of the most superb horse Lorna had ever seen . . . and since being brought to the encampment she had seen many fine horses and rode several of them, to the delight of the tribesmen, who admired spirit and good horsemanship.

Her eyes dwelt admiringly on the horse that had been sent to please the Prince Kasim. It had a gleaming golden coat and a sweeping mane and tail the color of sunlight. It had also a temper and lashed out continually at the two men who held it, its hooves glittering as wickedly as its eyes and teeth.

"Mon Dieu!" The Shaikh strode toward the horse and a hush fell over the crowd. Lorna found she was clenching her hands together, half in excitement, half in apprehension. She knew that Kasim would mount that beautiful, unbroken horse. Dare those slashing hooves, those wicked teeth, the rippling muscles beneath the satiny golden coat.

He took hold of the halter and the two Arabs backed away and left him alone with the golden stallion. He spoke coaxing, deep-throated words and forced it to turn and face the sun, so it wouldn't make any shadow. The horse reared up, neighing and lashing out, and was brought down with a firm tug on the rope. The next instant the Shaikh leaped upon the stallion's back and sat there grimly as it reared up again, pawing the air and causing such a clamor that horses in the nearby stockades became restless.

Lorna watched breathlessly as the rider matched his skill and mastery against the raw nerve of the horse. He sat the stallion and held him facing the sun, his knees locked high against the gleaming sides, his silk *kibr* clinging to his strong body as the fierce young stallion fought to unseat him.

There were no spurs on the rider's boots, no saddle on the horse. It was a battle of wills, and the Shaikh's white teeth locked in a smile of devilry each time he dealt with a trick that would have sent a less determined horseman flying to the dust. He would be the master and the stallion would know it if the battle continued all night.

There was sweat and foam on man and mount when with a loud snort the golden stallion swept his mane in the dust he had kicked up. With a sudden laugh the Shaikh leapt to the ground and did one of the most daring things Lorna had ever seen . . . he took the stallion's proud head in his hands and stared straight into the wickedly gleaming eyes. The animal could have bitten him, gashed his face wide open, but instead it twitched its ears, flicked the corn-silk tail, and then with a thrust of its muzzle nearly put its master's collarbone out of place.

A cheer arose from the crowd who had watched the battle of wills with a fierce intensity. Their fierce dark faces broke into smiles. Prince Kasim had made friends with the golden one!

As the horse was led away and the tribesmen clustered around the victor, Lorna slipped away unnoticed to the oasis, where she leaned against a palm tree in order to catch her breath after the excitement.

She was fully aware that Kasim had not been showing off. Nor had it been mere bravado that had made him put his face so close to the stallion. He had been mesmerizing the animal, and the wild, proud creature had responded . . . it had succumbed to the strange magic and power that made the Prince the man that he was.

Lorna stood alone among the palm trees, dappled by the apricot light of the dying sun. Suddenly a tremor shook her from head to foot. She had not felt so unnerved since the night he had brought her to his encampment. He had the power, the strength, the physical beauty to make people love him . . . Lorna wanted only to have him!.

CHAPTER EIGHT

IN the *grande tente* after dinner that night Lorna found herself acutely aware of the lithe good looks of the Prince. Pleasure in the golden stallion he had tamed gleamed in his eyes and there was a note of indulgence in his voice when he addressed her.

"I have a present for you," he said. "Come over here and let me give you these."

She glanced up from the French magazine she was idly reading. He was holding a long chain of pearls in his fingers, milkily agleam against the tanned skin of his hands.

"Come! Leave your book and let me see how you look in pearls."

This was the first time he had wooed her with jewelery, though there had been times when he had caressed the lobes of her ears and touched her slender neck as if he wished to see them adorned.

"I . . . I never wear necklaces," she said nervously. "They give me the fidgets."

She felt his eyes upon her, taking in deliberately the velvet tunic and silk trousers that made her more appealing than she wished to be in his company. She found the *babouches* difficult to keep on and her feet were bare and white in the deep pile of the carpet on which she lay with her magazine.

"I wish to see you in this necklace." His voice now held a note of command, and Fedjr the gazelle hound stirred against his knee. "Not you, boy. I speak to the *petite,* who knows I can make her obey me."

"What will you do?" she asked. "Put a rope around my neck and enforce my obedience?"

"A rope of pearls," he mocked. "Shall I order Fedjr to fetch you to me? He may well mistake those ankles of yours for a gazelle's."

"Brute!" She tossed aside her book and walked slowly across to him. She stood like a statue in front of the divan, but was pulled down beside him and forced to endure his touch as he placed the chain of pearls about her neck. They gleamed like satin and each one was perfectly matched.

"Cultured?" she murmured, daring his anger.

He smiled rather dangerously. "One day you will dare me too far, my girl. Each one of those pearls would keep an Arab family in food for months."

"Then please let your Arabs have them!" She went to remove the necklace, and at once his hand closed on her upraised arm. The amusement died out of his eyes and they glittered with all the tawny menace of a leopard's.

"If you remove the pearls I shall bruise your arm," he said through clenched teeth. "They are a gift from me, and you will not insult me by refusing to wear them."

Her own teeth were clenched, for his fingers were digging into her arm and hurting her. "Y . . .

you tyrant," she said. "You must always have your own way."

"Lamentable," he mocked. "Would you have me give my *kadin* a string of date stones?"

"D . . . don't call me that!" She felt choked by his pearls and by the word, which meant girl slave.

"You call me a tyrant."

"It applies!"

"Well?" He held her eyes. "Are you not my *kadin?*"

"You made me so, and I hate you for it!"

"The honey draws the bee, the flame the moth, the seductive woman the seduction of the man." Amusement glimmered again in his eyes. "Other women would be delighted to be chained by pearls."

"I am not other women." Her lips quivered and she glanced down at the pearls and wondered from whose neck they had been torn long ago. The design of the necklace was antique and quite beautiful. A woman could have looped them about her hair, her throat, and her waist.

"No, you are not like other women," he said. "Too many flaunt their charms. You I am discovering slowly, peeling the petals one by one from your secret heart." He touched her heart and ran his vibrant fingers across her throat. She lifted a hand as if to shield herself from his touch, and at once he saw the bruises on her bare arm.

"My doing?"

"Who else but you?"

"You bruise quickly, like a flower." He put his lips to the marks. "Let me hide them with a kiss, then with a bracelet."

From the carved box beside him he took a wide golden band set with blue gems. "Lapis lazuli," he murmured, and clasped her slender arm in the slave bracelet.

He studied her, decked in silk and his barbaric jewellery. His gaze traveled all over her to the arching bareness of her small feet. "There is a saying," his breath stirred warm against her earlobe, "that the rose remembers the dust from which it sprang. Are we not all primitive, even you with your cool skin and your eyes like blue flowers?"

She felt his touch right through the silk that covered her, his eyes held hers, burning with the desert fires that her coolness could not discourage.

"I wonder what you would be like, stirred into flame?" he murmured. "Shall I stir you to flame, *amiga?*"

His use of the Spanish endearment shook her. His face above hers, so darkly handsome, held her gaze and pierced her with its dark-lashed eyes, its mouth that was both passionate and a little cruel. She never touched him of her own free will, and she felt faint as there stole over her a sudden longing to touch his face tht was like a sculpture in warm bronze. She closed her eyes to shut out his face, feeling betrayed by her own inborn love of beauty. She felt his lips against her eyes. She heard him whisper to her in French. She trembled in his hard, warm embrace.

"I go now to see if the grooms have bedded my golden stallion for the night." He kissed her in the small hollow under her cheekbone. "He is a beauty,

98

eh? I might let you ride him when he is a little tamer. You would look well on him."

He arose before she could speak and went from the tent with the noiseless grace peculiar to him. The silence and the scent of sandalwood burning in the lamps settled around her. Her fingers plucked at the pearls and the lamplight shone in the blue jewels of the bracelet he had clasped about her arm. He was the strangest man. One moment he threatened and bruised her . . . the next he offered to let her ride the golden stallion.

She sank back against the cushions of the divan and let her weighted eyelids sink down over her eyes. Tomorrow he left for his friend's encampment and she knew that he intended to be away for several days. The thought was exciting. It sent a thrill of wildest hope running through her. She might, during those few days, find the opportunity to escape from this place at last!

His chain of pearls felt heavy about her slender neck. She longed to throw them off, but she dare not risk angering him again.

When he returned to the tent the night air had ruffled his hair, and she did not protest when he lifted her bodily from the divan. "You are sleepy, eh?" His eyes smiled down into hers. "Shall I carry you to bed, my little *bint*?"

Her heart beat furiously against his . . . for always at night she grew afraid of this handsome barbarian! She shrank from the smile on his lips, and the deep purr in his voice.

"We ride at dawn," he said as he set her down beside the bed on which lay a delicate sleeping shift.

"The Kaid is expecting to enjoy several days hunting, so I cannot take you with me."

She felt him looking at her and caught the note of warning in his voice . . . she guessed that the Kaid would not approve of his young friend's guest, whom he had taken from her own people as a falcon of the desert might swoop on a pigeon.

"Ahmed will be made to suffer if you do anything foolish," he added.

"I am sure Ahmed will watch my every movement with the eyes of a hawk," she said. "He has been given his orders, has he not? I am to be kept here until you grow tired of me."

A brown hand caught at the pearls that chained her. She was drawn close to him and subjected to a close, searching look. "You would not find it pleasant to be lost in the desert, Lorna. Vultures follow the lonely traveler, and there are Arabs who would sell their own sisters into the harems of men who are far crueller, and far less fond of soap and water than I am."

With a soft laugh he let her go and went into the alcove to wash his hands. Lorna gave a shiver as she removed the pearls and the bracelet and heard him humming a song he was fond of. She had to get away from him . . . at whatever the risk.

A few stars still burned in the sky when the Shaikh and his retinue set out on their journey, and the palm trees stood dark against the pale sky.

Lorna was wrapped in a riding cloack against the chill in the early morning air, and she and Kasim cantered a few yards ahead of his men. As they rode across the dawn-shadowed desert, the sands were

100

cool and the enchantment of it sent a thrill of wonder through Lorna. This was not the first time she had ridden *l'aube* with the man at her side, but today she would wave goodbye to him. . .perhaps for ever.

Her eyes beneath the encircling *shesh* were intense as violets, and she was glad that he rode silently beside her, absorbed in the desert spaces he loved beyond anyone.

Ahmed was among the cloaked Arabs who rode behind them. He would be left in charge of her, the master's trusted *aide-de-camp,* whose vigilance Lorna was determined to escape. Already a plan was forming in her brain. Tomorrow she would pretend to have a slight fever and would keep to her bed. During the siesta hour, when the entire camp was sheltering from the intense heat, she would rip open the back of the tent with the scissors she used for altering her Eastern garments and steal away on any horse that was available. She was now accustomed to the Arab horses, who were so swift on the wind that she had high hopes of getting away from the man who had captured her . . . made her a slave to his commands.

"You are quiet." She gave a start when all at once he spoke to her. "What are you plotting?"

Her heart raced. The man had an uncanny gift for reading her mind, a further invasion of the privacy and independence she had valued so much.

"The dawn light over the desert always leaves me spellbound," she replied. "It's so mysterious somehow — the way it must have been when Adam and Eve first saw it."

"Eternally the same and yet it never palls." The

keen, tawny eyes flashed over her *shesh*-encircled face, a pale heart within the yards of fine muslin. "As I have said before, the desert is like a woman, but only a very unusual type of woman never grows tiresome. Will you miss me when I am away from you?"

"Do you want an honest answer?" she parried.

"No." He gave a rather curt laugh. "I know you won't pine for me, but are you not curious to know if I shall miss my *bint* with the sunny hair and the stormy heart?"

"I daresay your friend the Kaid will offer distractions that will be far more to your liking. You are not a man of emotion, Prince Kasim, you are a man of action. To you I am a creature to be tamed. Once you have bowed my head. . . ."

"You know why I took you," he cut in. "You know why I keep you. In a white *shesh* you are like a sister to the dawn itself—see how it spreads like a blush, slowly, drowning the pale sands in softest pink."

It was a wonderful, awesome sight, for the rising sun was a curve of red-gold, spreading a radiance that outlined the sand hills and spilled violet shadows in the hollow places. The stars had almost faded, all but one that burned overhead as if transfixed in the golden sky.

Lorna's eyes shone. A love of the unusual ran in her blood and she thought of her father, painting such a scene during his sojourn in the desert. A sigh escaped her.

"For what do you sigh?"

"Oh. . . ." She avoided a meeting with his eyes. "For eggs and bacon and a cup of tea."

"You continually amuse me," he said with a laugh. They had set out on cups of coffee; now he wheeled his horse and for a moment man and mount were outlined vividly against the sunrise. He raised a hand and everyone halted. They would make camp for an hour, he informed them. He pointed at some sandstone rocks, carved by the desert winds into strange shapes. "The *lella* wishes to take breakfast in the desert."

The men glanced at each other. It was plain that they had not hoped for a break before mid-morning, and Lorna saw them smile and nod knowingly. More than once had she heard it whispered by them that the Shaikh was bewitched by her.

She glanced at him as they galloped toward the sandstone rocks and she remembered little confusing things about him. How he could often charm her with his conversation. How he would bring her a fluffy *saluki* puppy to play with, or come striding into the tent with a laughing brown child astride his shoulders. . . .

"I am rather hungry myself," he smiled. "It's our keen desert air."

When the rocks were reached, everyone dismounted and a tamarisk fire was soon alight and the coffee pots were set to heat. A large pan was unpacked and small lamb cutlets and onions were soon frying over the fire and emitting a mouth-watering aroma.

The Shaikh leaned against a rock a little distance from the campsite, a striking figure in his white robes and headcloth, with a dark blue cloak thrown back over one shoulder.

Lorna breathed the aroma of the food cooking over the tamarisk fire, and the spiciness that seemed to arise out of the pores of the desert. The rolling sands, the illimitable blue sky, and the tall man against the rocks blended to form a picture she would never really forget. A man who was as relentless and unpredictable as the desert itself.

She flicked her riding-whip at a bush, and then she stared as something crawled dark and crooked from a crevice in the rocks where the Prince lounged, head bent to the cigaret he was lighting. He was unaware of the crawling object, and Lorna knew that the thing so close to him was a black scorpion, whose sting was deadly.

It might sting the man and free her today . . . forever. All the vigorous life and vitality would be sapped out of his lithe and splendid body by the poison in the scorpion's sac. . . .

"Kasim," his name broke from her, "there's a scorpion crawling beside you!"

He saw it the instant she warned him and flicked his burning cigaret at it. The black thing fell to the ground and was crushed completely beneath his riding-boot, for even in its death throes a black scorpion could inflict a painful death.

Slowly he glanced up and gazed for a long, wordless moment at Lorna. "Why did you warn me? That ugly thing would have been a far more deadly agent than a badly aimed knife."

She shrugged and dragged her gaze away from his. Her fingers clenched her whip. "I shouldn't want my worst enemy to die in agony from the sting of a scorpion."

"You worst enemy is grateful." He came to her

104

in a single stride and took hold of her hand. The incident of the scorpion had escaped the notice of his men, but several pairs of eyes saw him raise Lorna's hand to his lips.

"Don't!" She snatched her hand from his.

A coffee pot fell with a crash from the hand of a startled Arab. No one defied the Prince Kasim, least of all a slip of a *bint*. But upon this occasion the master accepted the rebuff. . . he even smiled a brief sardonic smile.

They ate a tasty breakfast together, and then he said that he and his retinue would ride on. Ahmed would escort the *lella* back to the encampment.

He then drew Lorna to one side, shackling her wrist with fingers she could not escape from. "You must give me your word that you will not slip away from Ahmed and lose yourself in the desert. You have no real knowledge of how to fend for yourself in such a vast and dangerous place. Anything could happen to you."

"I'm already aware of that, *mon maitre*," she murmured.

"Little fool!" He seemed to check an impulse to shake her. "If I can't have your promise, then I shall have to take you with me and you will not enjoy being shut up with a lot of strange women while I go out hunting with the Kaid. Come, make your choice!"

At once Lorna saw her chance of escape slipping away from her and she looked quite desperate when she said to him: "I promise to be good! Please, don't force me to go with you . . . it would so embarrass me."

"Yes, I know how you feel." He tilted her chin

105

with his hand and searched her eyes. "That is the reason why I hesitate to leave you. You are impulsive—"

"I have learned, Prince Kasim, that your will is law," she broke in. "Will you be so cruel as to take me among people I don't know, as your English *bint* who hadn't the sense to keep out of the way of horse thieves, and—"

"*Gardez bien,* you had better not say it!" His hand gripped painfully. "Awhile ago you saved my life and I am in your debt. Return with Ahmed. Ride with him whenever you wish. The rest is with *le destin.*"

He drew away from her and straightened the folds of his cloak. There was a stillness about him that was not so much anger as resignation. Desert men believed deeply in *kismet* and Lorna knew that Kasim was no exception.

He gave the signal for everyone to mount, and after assisting Lorna into the saddle of her horse, he swung into his own saddle and gripped the reins with lean brown hands. His nostrils flared as he breathed the wild and spicy air. His tawny eyes flashed over the landscape, a shimmering ocean of sand, rising and falling in billows of beaten gold.

"The desert is not always so calm," he said to Lorna. "Very often such calmness is the prelude to a storm."

"It looks very wonderful at the moment," she said.

"Most of the things we think wonderful have an element of danger in them." His eyes held hers, and the straight black line of his brows intensified their brilliance. *"Au 'voir,"* was all he said, and she sat still and straight in the saddle as he rode off without looking back, leaving her in the charge of Ahmed. The riding cloaks billowed out in the desert wind and sand was thrown up in fine clouds beneath the hooves of the horses. Then she wheeled her own horse.

"Let us go," she said to Ahmed, and she saw from the sullen set to his face that he was not pleased at being left behind to look after her.

CHAPTER NINE

At the brush of her boot her mount was away like
the wind, but Ahmed's rawboned horse was not to
be outdistanced and he was at her heels as she
galloped into camp and slipped from the saddle
outside the *grande tente*. She caught at her *shesh*
and pulled it off, and her hair caught the sun and
seemed to hold it. "Put away my horse," she said to
Ahmed. "I . . . I feel a little tired."

He inclined his head, a sullen light in his eyes as
they rested on her face. As Hassan emerged from
the tent she added to her playacting. "How warm it
is." She pressed a hand to her forehead. "I . . . I
hope I'm not going down with a fever."

She entered the tent in a listless manner and
Hassan followed in some concern. "Can I get
anything for *madame?*" he asked.

"No." She dropped down on the divan and
leaned her head back. "I shall be all right. I may
have a touch of the sun."

"A *toubib* has arrived from Sidi Kebir, unaware
that the Prince Kasim would be away. Would
madame like to see him?"

"*A doctor?*" Her eyes met Hassan's in astonishment. "A French doctor?"

"Arabian, *madame.* He does much good work

at Sidi Kebir, where my lord's father is the Emir. He comes here to take a look at those who are sick, and who need to have teeth removed."

Lorna stared at the tips of her boots, deep in the pile of the carpet. She was putting on an act and did not feel feverish, but her cheeks grew hot at the thought of meeting this doctor. He might not be aware that an English girl was here in camp, and it rushed over her that she was not prepared to face anyone from the city where Kasim's father and sister lived.

"I don't need a doctor," she said. "I shall keep to the tent, Hassan, and please ensure that I am not disturbed."

Hassan gazed at her a moment in his inscrutable way, then he withdrew quietly, leaving her alone in the cool dimness of the tent. With a sigh she reached for a cigaret and lit it, and it was inevitable that the aroma should bring visions of the Shaikh. Why had she warned him about the scorpion? Its sting would have released her, yet she had hesitated, been appalled to think of that ugly black thing bringing to his knees the strong, arrogant desert man. She puffed smoke and told herself she was soft like most women, hating to see pain inflicted though she had to bear it herself.

As the day waned, she grew bored with the tent and its trappings. After a solitary dinner she wrapped herself in her cloak and made her way to the oasis. She was aware that a lean figure followed her as silently as a shadow and she fought the exasperation that boiled up in her. Why should the Shaikh care if she ran off into the desert and was not heard of or seen again? To him she was but a toy to adorn with a chain of pearls. A means of amusement at the end of his day . . . one more woman he would forget in an hour.

She found her favorite palm tree, with its reclining trunk that made it restful to lean against. The night was moonless and everything was still but for the rustling of the palm leaves, shaped so curiously like human hands. The starlight etched their gestures, and a few frogs croaked in the well.

When she caught the whiff of cigaret smoke and saw the pale gleam of a *burnous* she took the man for Ahmed. She was deeply startled when he spoke to her, in French with an accent as clipped as the Shaikh's.

"Do not be alarmed, *madame.* I have hoped to speak with you all day, but Hassan informed me that you did not wish to be disturbed. I am Omair ben Zaide." He gave her a courteous bow and she caught the gleam of curiosity in a pair of dark eyes. "I am a doctor and in the course of making my rounds of the camp I learned that my friend the Prince Kasim had a guest—a lady with wondrously fair hair."

She detected no hint of irony in the words, but her cheeks burned in the dimness. She felt a wild urge to rush away, but with an effort she subdued it.

"It must have surprised you, Doctor, to learn that his *guest* was English. I am sure that when you have been here before his tent has been the home of a girl of Araby."

There was an acute little silence and she saw the end of the doctor's cigaret glow brightly, revealing for a brief moment a lean face whose features were strikingly regular. Omair ben Zaide was far more Arabian to look at than his friend the Shaikh, but at the same time he looked far less haughty and commanding.

"When I have been here before, *madame,* Kasim has not been fortunate enough to have a pretty woman with him. I have been told by one of my patients, whose small child would have choked on a bead if you had not taken the imp by the heels and shaken her, that you have golden hair. Arabs see few people who are truly fair."

"That is beside the point, Doctor." She drew herself up and added icily: "Did your friend's people omit to tell you that he forces me to stay here? Do you fondly imagine that I am his willing companion? I detest the man!"

"Yet I have learned that you ride with him, that you practice archery together, and play chess. I am told, *madame,* that he treats you as an equal."

She gave a scornful laugh. "How does he treat his other women?"

"What other women?" asked Omair ben Zaide, a note of stiffness in his voice.

"Doctor, would you have me believe that before I came here he lived the life of a monk?"

"Not a monk, *madame.* He is a man of fastidious tastes."

"Your fastidious friend, doctor, thought nothing of throwing me across his saddlebow and riding off with me as if I were no more than a gazelle he had caught." The burning words were out, and she was able to give voice to them because it was dark and because this man was a doctor.

"Sometimes a man is blinded by beauty to what

111

is right. Kasim is the only son of a powerful Emir and I fear he is accustomed to having his own way."

"How can you make excuses for him?" she asked, frozenly.

"I admire him, and perhaps if I were not a doctor I might resort to riding off with a woman I—wanted." He dropped his cigaret end to the ground where it glowed a moment and then died. "To people who live in the desert, who are ruled by the sun and governed by a sense of fatalism, there is no tomorrow, *madame*. There is only today, the moment to be grasped as if it were a flower or a fruit. Desert people are called the children of the stars . . . they burn with the same incandescent force."

"Whatever they burn with," she said, "it is no excuse for altering the course of someone else's life to satisfy a passing attraction. The Shaikh whipped a man for stealing a horse, but I gather the same laws don't apply for stealing a woman?"

"It is true to say, *madame,* that my friend the Shaikh does make laws of his own." A tinge of amusement ran among the words. "He controls many wild tribesmen, so I suppose it is natural in him to control a young and lovely women. Can you say he has been cruel to you, *madame?*"

"He has not raised his whip to me," she said tersely. "But there are other ways of being cruel . . . he brought me here against my will!"

"I understand." Now she caught a brooding note in the doctor's voice. "To a man of any land a woman is one of life's adornments, to please the eye, to give solace from care. The cares of the Prince Kasim are not small ones. His father is not a

112

well man, and I think Kasim looks forward with regret to the time when he must give up the desert life he loves so much. He must in the course of time take his father's place, and perhaps it is because of his need to forget the inevitable that he turns to you, *madame*."

"And as a mere woman I must not mind that I have been snatched away from my own kind and forced to endure a life that is still very strange to me?" Lorna gazed at the enormous stars through the palm trees and remembered how she had wanted to pluck one in the garden of the Ras Jusuf . . . so long ago, and yet only weeks ago. From among the tents drifted the sound of Arabian music, a repetition of melody, a lament, and a barbaric plea, reminding her of the reed flute of the sand-diviner.

"It is to be expected of the desert that it brings out the primitive in people." A graceful spreading of the hands followed this observation of the doctor's. "But don't you find enchantment in the desert at dusk, the lighting up of the stars and the brushwood fires? Does not the desert dawn make you aware of the beauty hidden in the heart of the savagery?"

She met in the starlight the almond-shaped eyes of Omair ben Zaide. His robes fell in sculptured folds around his lean figure and he wore a *shemagh* that was very white against the darkness of his face. He was purely Arabian. The Prince Kasim was much bigger built, and only the skin of his face, throat, and arms was deeply bronzed. He liked the pleasure of kissing a woman on the lips, and Lorna knew that such a caress was foreign to the pure Arab.

113

A little shiver ran over her skin as she remembered the feel of his warm, demanding lips.

"Like everyone else," the words broke from her, "you think me honored to be the woman in the master's tent. I detest him for the slave he has made of me!"

"Slave?" Omair ben Zaide laughed softly. "You hardly strike me as a slave, *madame.* You speak your mind. You go among his people and make friends with them. You must be aware that they like you? They call you Theldja—white as snow. They think you as graceful as the little moon. They are not surprised that their Shaikh wanted you."

Again she shivered. She wanted only her freedom!

"Your friend may not have broken his own laws," she said, gathering her cloak around her, "but he has broken those I was brought up to respect. Don't you realize, Doctor, that he keeps me here as if I were some young tigress he enjoys taming!"

The doctor drew in his breath sharply, as if struck suddenly by the fact that she was an English girl who had not consented to her own abduction.

"Would it help, *madame,* if I said that fate plays a large part in all our lives? Things happen and we despair. Time passes and we realize that an unseen hand leads us in and out of the dangers and delights of the maze of life."

Omair ben Zaide leaned a little forward and held Lorna with his dark eyes. "Something beckoned you in the desert, eh? You followed and everything conspired to hold you there. Think back, *madame.* Those who hear the call of the desert hear it long before they see the reality."

It was true what he said, she had followed a strange and haunting call into the golden realms of the desert . . . but she hadn't dreamed that such a call would lead her into the captivity of a man who never listened when she asked for her freedom. Who commanded her obedience. Who charmed her or was stern, just as if she were a golden sand cat he kept for a pet! She would never forgive such arrogance!

"It grows late, Doctor," she said in a cool voice.

"I will escort you to the *grande tente, madame.*"

When they reached the great double-tent, she asked him in for a cup of coffee, but to her amazement he backed away from her as if stung. "You are kind, *madame,* but no." He shook his head. "Kasim would not be pleased if I took coffee alone with you at nightfall. It would not be proper, you understand?"

"He alone can ride over all the rules," she retorted. "What if I fall sick, Doctor? Will you be allowed to attend me?

"In my capacity as a medical man, of course." His teeth flashed in a smile. "In everything else I am Arabian."

"You believe in the veil and the *harem?*"

"I believe in respecting the household of a friend." He bowed politely. "I am very happy to know you, *madame,* and I hope we shall be friends."

"I hope so as well," she said, but was made doubtful by his loyalty to Kasim, who could do no wrong in his eyes. Everyone, even this charming, educated man, seemed bound to the Prince by

115

some deep and abiding bond of affection. "I'm a little tired, Doctor, so I'll bid you goodnight."

"Emshi besselema, madame."

He went silently away, wrapped in the white *burnous* that glimmered among the dark tents and then was lost. It has been a strange encounter, and they had talked so frankly because the darkness placed a mask over the face, and from behind a mask even the shyest person could speak about herself. Was that why these men of the desert liked their women veiled? Did the veil reveal the woman?

Lorna stood alone by the entrance of the tent, a slim, cloaked figure, reluctant to enter her lonely prison. At last she went inside and breathed the sandalwood, the lingering aroma of Turkish tobacco, and the saddle polish. These scents would always have the power to evoke her captor.

Hassan—the perfect servant—had left coffee simmering on the Primus stove, and on a tray there was a dish of honey cakes and almond fingers. She made a small supper and flipped through a magazine. It was French and there were photographs of some of the places she had seen with her father. Once they had dined at the Silver Tower and it was there she had tasted champagne for the very first time.

"May each bubble in your glass be a bubble of happiness," her father had said.

She sighed and wandered about the tent, only too aware that the Prince was away and yet keyed up to expect his sweeping entrance at any moment. He was so vital that he left part of his presence behind him. She could almost see his lounging figure on the black divan, a lean hand reaching forward to move a chess-piece, or to entwine itself in her hair, gently enough but with admiration gleaming in his tawny eyes.

Tawny as the desert itself!

One by one she put out the lamps, and the bead curtain clattered behind her as she entered the *harem*. It felt strangely cold tonight and she threw upon the ottoman bed the tawny leopard skin. Outside in the night a camel grunted, a fire hissed as someone damped it down, and then slowly the encampment settled down for the night.

Lorna lay wakeful in the low, wide bed, covered by the leopard skin, haunted by images that would give her no rest.

She turned from side to side, trying to shut out the dark and handsome face; trying not to hear his voice as he hummed *Après l'amour*. Trying not to feel him bending over her to see if she slept, touching with a fingertip a tear on her cheek, brushing it away with his lips and leaving his warm breath against her cheek.

She gave a little moan and pressed her face into her pillow. She had to get away! Dare she take the chance tomorrow? Early, before daybreak, while Ahmed still lay sleeping in his tent?

There were always spare saddles lying about, and bridles. She could fill a water-bottle from the bedside jug, and there were plenty of cakes left from her supper to take with her. Her heart beat fast. She knew that with the dawn she could escape . . . there was no one to stop her . . . no hard brown arm to imprison her, to hold her.

She stared into the darkness. She breathed the sandalwood. By this time tomorrow she might be again in Yraa, miles from the desert encampment.

She could barely wait for the night to pass . . . for dawn to come stealing into the tent and move lightly the bead curtain of the *harem*.

CHAPTER TEN

S<small>HE</small> was away and riding with the winds of dawn!

How easy it had been to creep from the tent like a shadow in the half-light, and take a horse, any horse, for no animal without speed and stamina was bred in the stockades of the Prince Kasim. The horse had been skittish at first, a fleet young mare with a saffron coat and white socks. She had spoken to it firmly, and now Lorna felt in perfect accord with the rhythm of her mount, whose pace was long and supple.

The dawn air was like wine, mingling with her sense of freedom to make her feel heady. She galloped headlong across the sweeping curves of sand, putting as much distance as possible between her and the camp, hopeful that the desert wind would soon erase the deep tracks her horse left in the sand.

What a wind! Cool against her face and her eyes, which had felt heavy after an almost sleepless night.

She laughed exultantly. She was free and she had not forgotten a single essential. She had water in a leather bottle, food in a satchel, a woollen cloak against the cold that always came with nightfall, and a muslin *shesh* to wrap about her head when the sun arose and burned over the desert.

She knew she was heading in the right direction, toward the hills of Yraa that were as yet pinpricks in the distance. She was not intimidated. She was riding swiftly away from the man whose frown could make her more afraid than all these endless stretches of sand and rock, and an occasional hovering hawk.

The light that was spreading over the sands had a lemony tinge, and she urged her mount to even greater speed. With daylight her disappearance from camp would soon be noticed. Zahra would take coffee to the tent and find her gone. She would raise the alarm and Ahmed would ride in pursuit of her; spurred on by his fear of the Shaikh he would leave no rock unturned, miss not a hoofprint with his hawk's eyes, race the heart out of his horse in his determination to find her. She would have to ride long and hard if she were to escape him.

The wind billowed her cloak, and scattered the sand over the tracks her mount was making. The wind was her blessed ally! It was covering up behind her, and in her relief she neither wondered nor cared that it was extra strong this morning and the sunrise strangely colored.

In the saddle Lorna found solace from her thoughts, and as the hours passed the spaciousness of the desert had a numbing effect on her nerves. By the time she took a brief halt, in order to rest her horse, she was feeling almost relaxed. She smoked a cigaret and held on tightly to the bridle of the mare . . . this time she was not running the risk of being stranded in the desert.

She gazed around her and saw that the sands were darkening in patches. She glanced up at the clouding sky and became aware of how still and quiet it was, so that the rustling of the sands seemed louder in the stillness.

"A woman is like the desert," the Shaikh had said on one of their rides together. "So many secrets dwell in the heart of each. Both give peace, but turbulence is never far away."

Yes, a secretive place. A person could dwell in it a lifetime and yet never reach the heart of it.

Holding on firmly to the bridle of her mount she peered ahead to the range of hills that she hoped to reach before nightfall. They were blue-etched by the desert atmosphere, so near and yet still so far away. She climbed into the saddle and once again the saffron mare reared up and wheeled about like a circus performer. Lorna gripped the reins and dug in her heels. She rapped out some of the words the Shaikh used on a skittish horse, and with a snort the mare settled down and broke into her supple gallop.

It was about half an hour later when sudden spots of rain fell on Lorna's face. Soon it was raining steadily and once or twice Lorna thought she heard thunder, far away, beyond the hills of Yraa.

A storm in the desert would be unnerving, but she would face anything rather than be caught and taken back to the man she had fled from. She couldn't bear the thought of his anger. She couldn't face any more the torment of being with him. She was not loved by him. She was merely amusing for a while . . . when the novelty palled, or when the duty to his father recalled him to Sidi Kebir, he would soon rid himself of her.

In running away like this she kept her pride. He had not quite humbled her and she could start life anew, somewhere far away from the betraying beauty of the desert.

The rainfall ceased abruptly, but the sky stayed overcast and the atmosphere was very sultry. The sand began to swirl about in small flurries, and in the distance a haze was veiling the hills that were Lorna's goal. She felt a nervous tightening in her throat. If a sandstorm should arise, then everything would be blotted out in a rage of dust that might last for hours, even an entire night—and she had made no provision for such a disaster.

The very thought was enough to spur her on, and she crouched low in the saddle and let the mare gallop at full speed.

The atmosphere grew gloomier and yet hotter with every passing minute, and Lorna began to feel as if a helmet of bronze was pressing down on her tired head. She heard a strange, wind-driven sound from across the desert spaces . . . a wailing that made her go cold despite the heat.

Her instincts warned her that the storm would come suddenly, and she looked around for somewhere to shelter when the winds began to whip the sands without mercy.

Not so far distant she saw a clump of boulders and headed her mount toward them. Surrounding them was a straggle of thorn-bushes, dark and patchy against the sulphur coloring of the sands, and she was thanking her stars for this promise of shelter when lightning flared livid across the landscape, not only startling Lorna but the mare as well.

The skittish animal shied and reared up suddenly, so high that Lorna was jerked out of the stirrups and the saddle before she could save herself. She went flying to the sands, where she lay breathless, and shocked as the mare gave a shrill neigh and went galloping off.

Lorna staggered to her feet and clutched a hand to the sharp pain in her shoulder. She cried out after the bolting horse, but her cries were snatched away by the wind and soon the frightened animal was lost in the dust haze, trailing its bridle and carrying away in the saddlebag the precious water and food Lorna had hoarded so carefully through the day.

She stood stricken, and then when the lightning flashed again she realized that she must reach the shelter of the rocks. There at least she would be out of the lashing force of the storm, for by now the wind was clutching at her cloak and sand grains were striking her face and eyes.

Teeth clenched against the pain in her wrenched shoulder, she made doggedly for the shelter of the rocks and bushes. She felt too shaken, too hurt, even too angry for tears. Kasim's warning rang like a knell in her spinning brain. "You have no real knowledge," he had said, "of how to fend for yourself in such a vast and dangerous place as the desert."

The words seemed to mingle with the thunder and the wind. In the lightning she seemed to see again the flash of his eyes . . . and then as she reached the scoop of sandy ground behind the rocks, everything whirled and she went suddenly as weak as a kitten. The winds roared, the skies darkened, and she fell into the darkness and felt the sand against her face. . . .

Everything was in a fog when at last she opened her eyes. The air was filled with the choking dust and there was a furnace taste in her mouth.

She remembered vaguely that she had collapsed to the sand, but now her shoulders rested against a boulder and someone was kneeling beside her . . . his face half covered by a *shemagh* of white linen, above which his eyes had a fierce glitter.

She was desperately thirsty, and her shoulder was throbbing with pain. Everything seemed like a nightmare, but the lip of the proffered water-bottle was real enough. She gulped gratefully at the water, and as her senses came back to her there came also the realization that the man's arm encircled her. She pulled away from him, her frightened eyes fixed on his cloth-veiled face.

"Quelle folie," he muttered, and then the *shemagh* was pulled away to reveal strong, sun-bitten features that sent a thrill of wonderment through Lorna. The face was too well-remembered; his voice when he spoke had a savage edge to it.

"So you would brave a sandstorm to escape me, eh? As soon as I received word from Ahmed that you had taken a horse and galloped off, I set out after you from the Kaid's encampment. I know you are not quite a little fool. I knew you would make directly for the hills above Yraa, where you were staying at the Ras Jusuf."

His eyes held hers, stern and brilliantly tawny. "I might in my haste have passed these rocks had I not seen your *shesh,* caught and held by a thorn-bush."

He gazed at her for the longest time; into her eyes that looked like bruised flowers. "Foolish child," he said. "You might have known I would come looking for you. You might have guessed I would find you."

"I sometimes think you are Lucifer himself. . . ." Then she gave a shudder of pain. "My . . . my shoulder seems to have something amiss with it. The lightning frightened my horse and I was thrown . . . oh, it does hurt!"

He took hold of her and felt around her shoulder as gently as possible. "You have put out the bone," he said. "I can adjust it, *petite,* but to do so will hurt you."

She looked at him through the fog of whirling sand, and because everything had gone so wrong for her, she said tiredly: "Hurt me, Prince Kasim. You have done so before without letting it trouble your conscience."

He held her, his face like a bronze mask, and then he took a cigaret-case from his robes and placed one between her lips. A match flared and he put it to the tip. "A smoke will help the pain . . . are you ready?"

She took a deep pull on the cigaret and nodded. Her groan of pain was lost in the howling of the wind as with an expert movement of his hand the Shaikh jerked the dislocated bone back into its socket. She trembled with reaction and a cold sweat broke out on her forehead. A numbness followed the pain, which he said was caused by pressure upon a nerve. With lean, strong fingers he massaged her shoulder and arm until the life seeped back into them.

"Try moving it," he murmured.

She obeyed. "It aches, but I can tell the bone is back in place. Th-thank you."

"You have nerve, Lorna." He brushed the damp, sandy hair out of her eyes. "Soon now the sandstorm will grow into a monster with many lashing tails and we might be buried beneath the sand. Does it frighten you that when this storm is done, we might lie forever in each other's arms, with these rocks as our desert monument?"

She rested against the boulder and finished her cigaret. She saw that his black horse Caliph was firmly hobbled and tethered, and that it hung its head to avoid the cut of the flying sand. The wind whipped Lorna's hair, and she tried to ignore the touch of warm hands as they bound her white *shesh* about her face and neck.

"It was folly to run away and risk being caught in a sandstorm," he said roughly.

"It was a greater folly to suppose I could get away from you." She looked at him and heard the wailing of the wind. "The desert takes care of its own, and you are as relentless as the desert."

"You burn my heart," he mocked. "I find you like a snowflake lost in hell, and you have not a single kind word for me."

"Since when, Prince Kasim, did you ever want kindness from me?" She looked at him with grave blue eyes. "When did you ever give it?"

He frowned, and then turned his head so that

his profile was outlined against the sand haze. "There is no *tendresse* in a desert storm, eh? It is all danger, and we are very much alone in it."

"How long will it last?"

"Who can tell? *Le destin* alone."

"And when it is over?" She crushed out the end of her cigaret in the sand. "One day you must let me go must I be completely humbled before you do so?"

Whatever his answer she never heard it, for in that moment there was a terrific roar and as the sand swirled about them, stinging and maddened by the wind, he wrapped her in the heavy folds of his cloak and drew the hood right over them, holding her close and hard against him.

She fought silently the fear of him that swept over her, and then she subsided and buried her face in his shoulder, lost with him beneath the driving, choking clouds of sand.

It was like a hurricane and Lorna heard the bushes being torn up and the smaller rocks flying in the wind. A demented wind, holding a shriek that tore at her nerves, that deafened and almost made her want to break into tears.

"It is all right." The words were a comfort but every now and again he shifted their position, for the sand was piling up on them. Once when she gave a little moan of distress, he pressed his lips to her temple.

His lips were warm, rough with sand, and as her eyes closed there swept over her a feeling of weakness that had nothing to do with the storm. She lay helpless in his arms, crushed, breathless, smarting from the sand grains, yet she felt the oddest contentment stealing over her. The sand might bury them together. They might lie locked in an eternal embrace . . . like lovers in a myth.

"Lorna?" There was a note of urgency in the voice so close to her ear. "Can you breathe . . . are you all right?"

"Kasim . . ." She spoke drowsily. "I have the strangest feeling. . . ."

"Come, you must not fall asleep!" He shook her and sand fell in upon them. Raging billows of sand, smothering them, grilling them alive in a furnace of choking dust and heat.

She forced open her eyes and found his face close to her own. Her lips parted, his lips crushed them and drew away. "You must not fall asleep," he said again, fiercely.

"Kasim . . . how long will it last?"

"I don't know, little one." He held her within the protective arch of his chest, so close that she felt his heart beating. "Be brave."

"I . . . I always try to be."

"Yes, always you tilt your chin and look a man straight in the eye. Ah, such a wind! A storm of the devil!"

"Your poor horse!"

"Yes." He spoke somberly. "We must hope that the poor beast does not become crazed by all the sand . . . he may break his tether."

"We would be stranded."

"Quite stranded." The strong hands found the slimness of her under the cloak. She shuddered at her own depth of response to his touch.

"It is all right." He spoke curtly. "I am merely loosening your garments in order to help your circulation. I am not quite a monster of cruelty, if that is what you are thinking."

She couldn't speak. She was helpless beneath the onslaught of feeling that swept her. She knew in this tortuous, storm moment that she responded to his touch because she belonged to him. Heart, soul, and spirit she belonged to this man of the desert, and she had not fled from him but from the love she felt for him.

He had made her love him! He had invaded her heart and mastered her with the laugh of a tamer.

He had left a knife to her hand that first night in his tent . . . he might well have left her alone to see if she would try and escape him.

Loving him . . . hating him for playing with her as a tamer might play with a young tigress, she fought the fascination that swept over her. "Can you wonder that I think you a brute?" she gasped.

At once she felt the crush of his arms, and the next moment she realized that he was shielding her as a great cloud of sand struck at them, making it impossible for them to see or hear or even to think. They were deafened, smothered by a blinding wave of dust.

For seconds . . . minutes . . . hours they were lost in the whirlpool of sand, and then came a silence like a clap of doom, a thunderous stillness, and Lorna felt a rising panic as her breath seemed choked off.

With an oath, and using every ounce of his terrific strength, the Shaikh strained upward until some of the sand began to shift. Again and yet again, until Lorna felt drops of perspiration fall from his face on to hers. Gasping and dizzy she tried to help him, and then his head and shoulders broke open the barrier of sand and the blessed air rushed in. He used his arms to cleave more space and pulled Lorna out into the open.

They lay gasping and gulping the air, the sand in their eyes, up their nostrils, and down their throats. All around them a strange stillness brooded . . . a spellbound silence after the rage of the storm. A tremor ran through Lorna and all at once tears of reaction were streaming down her face and making grooves in the grit that clung to her skin.

Kasim rose to his feet and went to his horse. He spoke soothingly to the shivering animal and brushed off the sand that clung to the patches of sweat. His own face looked devilish, for sand had crusted in the lines beside his mouth and his eyes. "Thank *le bon Dieu* we still have the horse," he said. "It would have been no picnic to be stranded in the desert with a bottle of water between us and many miles to cover to the encampment."

Lorna linked the tears from her lashes, still too dazed to grasp the full meaning of the words. Across the wastes of sand rustled a sharp night wind. All warmth had died out of the day. The heavens were dark, and over a high rim of sand came the howling of a jackal.

The Shaikh bent over Lorna with the water-bottle and urged her to drink. The water washed the grit from her teeth and eased her dry throat. He took a swallow himself and all the time he looked at her. "I think we will rest here for the night and start back for the encampment early in the morning."

"The encampment?" she echoed.

"Yes." His voice took its knife edge again. "You are coming back with me whether you want to or not."

She pulled off her *shesh*, gritty with sand, and the night wind ruffled her hair and soothed her eyes. "Why bother with me when I have spoiled your hunting and hawking with your friend the Kaid? I am but a woman . . . easily replaced."

"Yes, you are but a woman." He drew her to her feet and held her elbows in a firm grip. "But I am not yet ready to let you go — not yet, my bit of ice. I have not yet known the pleasure of making you melt. Until then we stay together—*Inshallah.*"

"That expression is out of place!" She was on the defensive, still very shaken by her inward joy at being with him; of knowing he still wanted her. "You obey only your own will, Prince Kasim."

"You address me as if we were slave and master," he mocked. "Say my name without the preface."

"The storm is over," she said. "If I said it then, it was out of fear."

"Say it now . . . now when the wind is still and I am not fighting to keep both of us from being buried."

"Kasim. . . ."

"It sounds a little strange on your English tongue." He smiled and his arms closed around her. She was tense in them, fighting not to betray the delight that swept her. Man without a heart! It made no sense that her heart should race at his touch.

"We must rest for a few hours," he said, "and you must keep warm. Our desert climate is a

131

strange one, eh? So warm one minute, so cold the next . . . just like a woman."

His warm breath stirred against her cheek. "No—don't," she said, afraid of what her reaction would be to his kiss.

"One day, my girl," his laugh had a savage ring to it, "I shall wring a different cry from you. The English have a certain weakness, you know. They end by loving their enemies."

"Love?" She was fighting him and her betraying heart. "I don't know how you dare to use the word when it has no meaning for you."

"If I ever loved you, *mon ange,* I would frighten you to death. Little icicle, you have no conception of what a fiery love is like between a man and a woman."

"How would you know?" she fought back. "You have never loved anyone."

"I love only the desert, eh?"

Laughing, he released her and made for some tamarisk bushes that had been half torn out of the ground. They were woody-stemmed and soon ignited into a cheerful blaze. After settling his horse for the night the Shaikh came and settled himself beside the crackling fire. Lorna turned her head nervously when once again a jackal howled in the darkness beyond the circle of firelight.

"Don't be afraid." A burning twig lit the handsome face as he applied it to his cigaret. "The jackals won't come close while we have a fire."

"They sound so—hungry." She drew her cloak close around her. "And the desert is so dark beyond the firelight."

"The storm clouds have veiled the stars." The

end of his cigaret glowed and darkened. "Come, rest against my knee and try to get some sleep."

She felt weary and her eyes were sore from the sand. It would be good to lie down, and after a slight hesitation she did as he suggested and rested against him. She was sleeping and yet acutely aware of their isolation. The tamarisk smoke mingled with that of his cigaret . . . his warmth began to steal into her.

Suddenly he glanced down and captured her gaze. "Are you not asleep yet?"

"It's all so strange . . . we might be the only two people alive in all the world." She felt lost in his tawny eyes, so brooding and yet so vigilant in the glow of the fire.

"Adam and Eve." A smile glimmered deep in his eyes. "The desert has been called the Garden of Allah, and there is something of Eve in most women."

"She was a temptress," Lorna murmured.

"So?" He quirked an eyebrow and his gaze held hers. "We are alone together under the veiled stars, and if you don't go to sleep very soon, I shall begin to think that you are tempting me to kiss you."

She held her breath, for if he kissed her and she melted to his touch . . . she turned her face quickly away, as if to avoid his lips, and she heard him laugh softly, mockingly.

His shoulders rested against a boulder, and the heavy folds of his cloak made a tent around Lorna. The fire crackled, and in a while she gave way to the languor that crept over her. She drifted off to sleep, sheltered by the man she had fled from . . . only to find herself back in his arms again.

CHAPTER ELEVEN

THE sandstorm had been so violent that it had wrought odd changes in the layout of the land. It was as if a giant had scattered the sandhills into a new pattern, and Lorna watched as Kasim took a keen look around him and she guessed he was judging the direction they should take from the rising sun.

She took a look at the hills behind them. In that direction lay Yraa and the place might have lain a thousand miles away for all she cared right now. She tilted her head and the sun seemed to catch in her hair. A thrill like no other ran through her as she felt a pair of tawny eyes upon her. "Our way lies south," he said sardonically.

His eyes had a burnished glint as she met them. What would be his reaction, she wondered, if she said that she wanted to go south, and wanted never again to look back toward the cool north? But it was something she must keep to herself. This complicated man of the desert liked a challenge, and while she challenged him she was sure for a while of a place in his life.

"You seem unsure of the terrain," she said. "What if we get lost?"

"I would always choose to be lost with you."

His smile was wicked. "Your hair robs the sun—it is amazing that you look so fresh after the storm and a night spent in the desert."

She swept her eyes over his unshaven face, and he fingered his jaws with a rueful grin. "You might well look superior, you little madam. Any impudence from you and I shall —" He took a step toward her and she backed against his black horse, who jibbed and jangled his harness. She gave a half-laughing gasp, feeling a joy that ravished her as Kasim caught hold of her and bent her over his arm.

She was slim, pliant in her breeches and shirt, shuddering in his arms as he looked at her, his eyes desert gold beneath his tousled black hair.

"I could break you in half and discard the pieces," he said in a soft, taunting voice. "I could make you tame to my hand, if I wanted to."

"Only because I've had no breakfast and I'm feeling weak," she quipped back at him, with spirit.

His teeth showed in a smile as he gazed into her eyes that were like blue flowers opened wide by the sun. He drew her suddenly hard and close to him, and she knew in her bones that he had a need of her which he would never admit to. His life of leadership admitted of few relaxations . . . with her he was able to let down some of the barriers that his position imposed on him. He wanted no submissive slave. He wanted her, with her blaze of fair hair and her skin that contrasted softly white with his. He wanted her and she was his, with or without the love she might have got from a man more civilized.

As he kissed her half-parted lips, she could have

died with longing, with love, with fear of the future. His lips caressed her cheek and the side of her neck and she felt his bristles. "Come, *ma fille,* we had better be on our way!"

He released her and turned to the horse to make sure all was well with the spirited stallion. Half their water had gone to the horse, who must carry both of them across many miles of desert beneath the hot sun. The great horse tossed his mane at the touch of his master's hand. He nuzzled the broad shoulder and gave a nicker of love.

Lorna watched them as she adjusted her *shesh,* and she remembered what the Shaikh had said about caring more for his horses than the women who crossed his path. How many women had there been? He was so vital and handsome that Lorna could hardly bear the thought of the lovely Arabian girls he must have held in his arms. He was, after all, the son of a powerful Emir. A prince in his own right.

With a resilient bound he was in the saddle of his horse. "Step into my stirrup," he said to Lorna. She obeyed and was encircled by his arm and swung up in front of him. She felt the steely clasp of his arm and for a moment his eyes held hers. "I shall not let you go," he said.

"Poor Caliph," she said, and her heart was racing as she wondered if there had been a double meaning in his words. "He must carry our combined weights."

"You weigh no more than a palm bough." Suddenly his nostrils flared as he drew in the desert air. "This is not the first time I have carried you across the sands on Caliph's saddlebow!"

Then they were away, and this time she tingled with enjoyment of the ride. The sky was a wild apricot color, the sands had a velvety look in the distance The wind that whipped at them was exhilirating. Never had she felt so vividly alive and aware of the ruthless beauty of the desert. The hills of Yraa receded behind them and Lorna did not look back

Halfway through the day they met with a band of nomads who greeted them in a friendly way and were only too happy to give them water. As the sun was high, they were invited into one of the wide-open tents and food was offered them. Lorna was famished and she ate like any Arab, scooping up the meat and gravy with a flap of bread.

She would have been sent to eat in the women's section of the tent, but the Shaikh told these people she was a boy, lost with him in the sandstorm the night before. "Hungry but shy, with not much to say for himself." The gleam in the tawny eyes was full of devilment, but as caravan tea was being served to them, he whispered to her not to remove her *shesh*. "No Arab boy ever had soft golden hair," he said wickedly.

The tea was sweet with sugar and green with mint, but Lorna was dry and she drank several glasses and then drowsed against a big pillow stuffed with sheep's wool. She listened sleepily to the men talking together in deep-throated Arabic. They were rugged but kind, and when the Shaikh said at last that he and the "boy" must be on their way, the normads pressed upon them a goatskin of water, some bread flaps and a lump of cheese.

The sun was smoldering in the west when they set out again, painting the sands with color as they rode away from the low black tents. *"Allah ibarek,"* echoed behind them, and soon all was silence and they were riding in the afterglow of the desert sunset.

Make a sunset wish, Lorna thought, and it will be granted. But she made no wishes. Like these people of the golden sands, she was beginning to believe in *kismet*. What would be, would be. Everything was written in the sands.

Her head rested against the strong shoulder of the man she could not resist. His profile was hawklike against the luminous light that spread fleetingly across the desert. She would never betray what she felt for this man, to whom love for a woman was a lesser thing than his love for the desert, his horses, his tribe, and his elderly father who would one day recall him to Sidi Kebir.

Darkness came and the heat of the day vanished in coolness. There was a splendor about the stillness and the stars, so many of them that several were seen to fall, tiny golden comets that fell into space and flickered out.

Kasim's thoughts seemed lost in those starlight spaces, and Lorna left him to his silence. In a while he asked her if she was hungry. She shook her head and asked if they were nearing the camp.

"Another hour," he said, "and we will be there."

"Are you following the stars?" she inquired.

"Yes. Tonight they sparkle like gems, eh? One could almost reach up and pluck a handful."

"I would be content with one," she said.

"Of course you would." His smile was teasing.

"You are the girl who shrinks from being decked in pearls. Do you wish that what I told the nomads was true? Would you sooner be a boy?"

"If I were a boy—"

"You would not have caught my ruthless eye." He laughed, a deep purring sound in the dark. "As I said at the camp of the nomads, no boy ever had hair like corn silk."

"After all that sand last night it needs a good tubbing." Her cheek against his shoulder was warm. A boy indeed! Never had she felt so glad that she was a woman, and one he found attractive. "I can't wait to get into a bath of hot soapy water."

He laughed again. "You are a fastidious little cat, and perhaps that is why I like you."

What, she wondered wistfully, would an expression of *love* sound like from him?

They rode into camp amid a tumult of greetings from the men and women who came hurrying from the tents. Lorna was lifted down off Caliph and she quickly escaped from the confusion into the *grande tente,* which now felt more like home than any other place she had ever known. She kicked off her boots, ran her fingers through her sandy hair, and was thirstily drinking limoon when Zahra came to her.

"We were all so worried." The girl caught at Lorna's hand and pressed it to her cheek. "Why did the *lella* ride off and leave the *sidi?*"

Because the *lella* has less sense than a she-camel." Lorna shook sand grains out of her shirt, "Zahra, I must have a bath!"

"Instantly." The girl smiled, but she didn't leave at once to fetch the water. *"Lella?"*

"Yes, my dear?" For some reason Lorna felt the sudden grip of tension.

"A message came from Sidi Hebir while my lord was away—his father the Emir is sick. He asks for the Prince Kasim."

Lorna stared at the girl and her eyes were like pools of violet-blue shadow in her suddenly pale face.

"Will the *lella* go to the palace with my lord Kasim?"

Lorna's heart beat wildly. "I . . . I should not think so, Zahra. He will leave me here in camp . . . or he may send me back to Yraa. Is the Emir very sick?"

"I think so, *lella*. The Emir Mansour is quite elderly, though the Prince Kasim is a young man. Men of the East often marry very young women, and the Emir's wife was many years younger than he. She was a *roumia,* only with raven dark hair. She died when her son was thirteen and about to become a man."

"At thirteen he became a man?" Lorna's smile was grave and tender. "In my land he would have been a schoolboy, playing football and getting into all sorts of scrapes." Lorna's hands clenched at her sides. "Please fetch my bathwater, Zahra. I must wash off this sand . . . we were caught in the storm last night . . . it was only by the merest chance that the Prince Kasim found me."

"The *lella* must have been very glad?"

Lorna met the Arabian girl's eyes, so limpid and yet so wise. "Yes, I was glad," she said quietly.

As the flap of the tent fell into place behind the young Arab girl, Lorna at once sank down onto a divan and hid her face against the cushions. She was dizzy from shock, and her heart was aching. The Emir needed his son, and Kasim would go to him as soon as possible! She would not be asked to go with him.

Kismet. Now when she desired nothing else but to be with him, he was called away.

She had bathed and was seated on the foot of the bed, wrapped in a big towel and brushing her damp hair, when the bead curtain parted and Kasim entered in his imperious way. He too had bathed and was clad in a soft linen *kibr* open at the throat, his hair was darkly agleam, but his eyes were somber as Lorna glanced up at him.

"Hassan is bringing our supper," he said. "Do you feel more relaxed after your bath?"

The scent of her bath still clung to the room and to her person, and she was acutely aware of his attraction and her own defencelessness. "I . . . I have to get dressed," she said.

"In one moment." He sat down beside her and took the brush from her hand. To her confusion he began to brush her hair, which was as soft and shining as an infant's after its tubbing.

"If we parted for ever tonight," he said, "I should remember always the soft feel of your hair and the way it holds the desert sunshine."

Though her heart ached at his words, she yet found the courage to spar with him. "This is a new role, Prince Kasim, valet to your slave girl."

He dropped the brush and gripped her shoulders. "My father lies ill at Sidi Kebir, and I leave at dawn to be with him, Lorna."

"I am sorry about your father." She spoke sincerely, and she longed to smooth the lines of worry from his face. "I hope his illness is not a grave one."

"He has suffered a heart attack. Lorna—"

"Yes, my lord?"

She addressed him quite naturally in that way, but he looked at her as if he thought she was being ironical. "You realize that I have to come to a decision with regard to . . . you?"

"Of course." She hardly dared to meet his eyes in case she betrayed her longing to be with him. Her pride was a forgotten thing, lost in the love that had found its place in her heart. She didn't want to be parted from him! Out of a wild fear had grown a tender love.

His face was stern, thoughtful, and then with a sigh he rose to his feet and towered over the bed. "We must discuss the matter, but for now I will leave you to dress. Don't be too long, will you?"

She shook her head with a slight smile, but the smile soon faded as he left her and she began to dress in the garments that no longer felt strange. Her tunic was a soft rose color over organza trousers, and this might be the last time she would wear them to please the Shaikh.

She stood hesitant a moment at the bead curtain, then she quietly joined him in the outer tent. His back was to her, so that for a moment she was free to let her gaze roam his wide shoulders, his proud dark head, the lean grace of him.

He swung around and their eyes locked. She knew she looked cool and composed, but it was a brave facade behind which she was hiding her love,

142

her fear of separation from him. No longer was her freedom worth anything to her. She wanted always to be his captive.

"Our supper is ready and it looks very tasty," he said. "Are you hungry? You should be after all those hours in the desert?"

"The food smells delicious." She sank down among the big cushions of the divan and felt him close to her as he served her with tender chicken spiced with herbs, and vegetables cooked in butter. "If Hassan were not so devoted to his master," she smiled, "I am sure he would win fame and fortune as a chef in a swank hotel."

"After a man has lived in the desert he finds it hard to breathe freely in a city."

"You hate the thought of leaving the desert, don't you?" She fought to keep her voice cool and impersonal. He mustn't know how she clamored to comfort him.

She felt the brooding flick of his eyes. In a corner of the tent a *brasero* glowed warmly. The entrance of the tent was firmly closed. They were alone, their intimacy was complete and at the same time so threatened.

"If my father dies I shall no longer be free to live in the desert, no longer be able to enjoy the life of the tribesmen." His left hand clenched on the table. "In the desert a man is but a man. He is close to the primitive heart of things, and often very close to danger. He can ride, hunt, be free of the shackles imposed on the city dweller. I would give any-thing —"

There he broke off and shrugged in a fatalistic way. Lorna finished the sentence in her own mind.

He would give anything to be as free as Ahmed or any of the men who rode and hunted with him.

They finished their supper and were left quite alone after Hassan came with their coffee. Tonight, Arabian coffee, which seemed redolent of all the essences of Araby. Lorna welcomed its richness, just as she welcomed the clamor of her love for the Shaikh, who now prowled about the tent with the soft, strong tread of a leopard.

A restless light burned in his eyes. His tall figure threw a long shadow in the lamplight, and as soon as he crushed out one cigaret he lit another.

Lorna associated none of his restlessness with her own dilemma. The touch of splendor about Kasim couldn't blind her to his dedication to duty. She told herself he would send her away without a qualm. She was but his toy . . . curled down among the divan cushions, silk clad, wearing the pearls he had given her, her fingers toying with them.

Suddenly he swung to face her with a gesture of controlled violence. Through narrowed eyes he studied her on the divan, the way her slender neck curved out of the rose silk, the way her small feet arched in ruby slippers. His own body grew forbidding in its stillness.

"Of what are you thinking?" he demanded. "You sit there so quietly, as if my departure tomorrow had nothing to do with you. Are you secretly glad that I am going? Can't you wait until dawn to see me ride away?"

She was unable to answer him. She was too stricken, too numb with pain, the tears like barbs of ice in her throat. He mustn't know how deeply she

144

cared, how torn she would be when he rode away on Caliph, his cloak flaring out above the gleaming black haunches of the horse, a vivid etching against the sunrise.

"Lift your lashes!" He came to her in a stride. "Look at me!"

She dared not, and shrank against the cushions as his hands encircled her throat and tilted back her head until he could look into her eyes. His hands were warm, sun-dark against the soft pallor of her skin.

"Chained!" He caught his fingers in the pearls as if to break the chain, and then he gave a low and savage laugh. "But tomorrow you go free, eh? I leave freedom for the chain of office!"

His look, his touch, the way he spoke, they all combined to hurt her. "I thought you intended to sell me to the next rich Arabian," she said in a choked voice.

His look grew smoldering beneath the level line of his brows. The next moment he was beside her on the divan and she was dragged into his arms, crushed and kissed with a violence that frightened her even as it thrilled her. "You thought I would let you go, eh?" He held her against the cushions and traced the pale gleam of her skin through the rose silk, touched the sheen of her hair in the lamplight. "Your eyes are the blue of the jasmine that grows in the garden of the palace, and you will see it growing in great clusters over the walls and pergolas beneath the windows of my apartments there."

She gazed up at him and saw a nerve beating hard beside his lips so near to hers. Lips that shaped words she didn't dare to believe in.

"Do you hear me?" His eyes smoldered. "I am taking you with me to the palace."

"The palace?" she echoed.

"My father has heard of you. He commands me in his message to bring with me the woman I have in my tent."

"You. . . ." She went weak in his arms. "You are not sending me back to Yraa?"

"I am sorry, my *bint.*" A mocking little smile played about his lips. "Not often does my father command me to do a thing, and because of his illness I don't wish to oppose him. You will come with me when I leave at dawn tomorrow."

"And then what?" she whispered.

"Who can tell?" He arose with supple grace from the divan and went to his desk. He unlocked a drawer and took something from it. He returned to her, raised her hand and found the finger that the star sapphire ring would fit. She gazed at him, not at the sapphire.

"The single star you wished for," he said.

"Will your father expect your *kadin* to be well adorned?"

His teeth flashed in a smile and she sensed a slackening of the tension that had vibrated in him all the evening. He encircled her with his arm and bent his head to drop a kiss in the crook of her elbow. "Do you like the ring, *ma fille?*"

"It's very beautiful."

"Less so than the woman who wears it." His lips caressed her earlobe. "Shall I make you melt, my ice-maiden? Shall I make you respond to me?"

"If I responded, then you would grow tired of me. You said so."

"So I did." He laughed lazily and fondled the tendrils of soft hair at the nape of her neck, sending little flame-like thrills through her . . . thrills she tensed against.

"How long have we been together?" he murmured. "Sometimes for me it seems but a very few days."

She closed her eyes as his lips stole to her lips. She told him how long it had been, lost, drowning in the delight that for him was surely a thing of the moment.

"Our desert air seems to agree with you, Lorna. I have not known you to be indisposed in any way. You would tell me, of course?"

"Concern, Prince Kasim, for me?"

His eyes were leopard-drowsy as they dwelt on hers. "You are but a girl," he said. "Naturally there have been times when I have been a little worried about you."

"Only a little?" She forced herself to speak lightly.

"I like to see you glowing and lovely—a sick creature on my hands would not please me."

"What a brute you are!" Her fingernails curled against his cheek. "A cruel abductor of innocent girls?"

"Only of one, *chérie!*"

"Did you twist all the others around your fingers like silken threads and have no need for force?"

"I am not forcing you right now." His eyes dwelt in her face, a pale heart against the purple velvet of a cushion. "You lie in my arms quite willingly."

147

"I only get bruised when I fight you."

He fondled the slender arm on which the slave bracelet gleamed. "You are so soft-skinned that I have only to breathe on you. Such soft skin, but an ice crystal for a heart."

"Would you want it otherwise?" She gazed at him through her lashes and her heart beat warm and fast with love of him.

He laughed, deep and purringly. Then he lifted her in his arms and carried her through the bead curtain to her couch. "You must get some sleep, Lorna. We leave for Sidi Kebir early in the morning."

She was wildly glad to be going with him, and yet at the same time apprehensive. At the palace she would have to meet his family. His father the Emir, and his sister Turqeya. What would they think of the English girl he took there as his guest?

He stroked her hair back from her eyes, soft as a child's in its fairness in the lamplight. "Say now, Lorna, if you would rather not come with me to the Emir's palace."

"Have I a choice, Kasim?" She felt the caress in his fingertips and hoped wildly that he would say she had no choice; that she was his to take with him, come what may.

"If I say that you are free to choose, then of course you will ask for a guide to take you to Yraa. But have you thought, *petite,* that your sudden reappearance will cause comment and speculation? No matter what excuses you make, what explanation you dream up for having vanished into the desert for weeks, people are bound to guess that you have been with a man." He smiled but she saw a question in his eyes. "You may wish of course to tell them I forced you to stay with me."

"People will have to think what they like." She spoke bravely, but the thought of being parted from him, of being alone and at the mercy of gossip was almost more than she could secretly bear.

"If on the other hand," he said deliberately, "you come to the palace of the Emir Mansour, then the mere mention of his powerful name will silence all the tongues that will wag in Yraa when you reappear looking so suntanned and lovely. As the guest of the Emir you will be beyond reproach."

"As the guest of Prince Kasim . . . ?" She smiled as her heart grew light again. "I suppose as your guest I would be extremely suspect?"

"I am a young man. It would be assumed that I had been—your lover!"

She couldn't look at him when he said *lover* in such a low and deliberate voice. She couldn't trust her own reaction to his sun-bronzed face so near to her, his dark tousled hair, his tawny eyes that the lamplight seemed to soften.

"We know the truth about that," she said. "It made me mad to be denied my freedom, Kasim, but I wouldn't let anyone call you a rake."

"You used to say that I was hateful," he murmured with a smile.

"You saved my life yesterday, so I can't very well go on hating you. That would be most ungrateful of me."

"Will you let me save your reputation by taking you to Sidi Kebir?"

"I must admit," she lowered her lashes in case

there was a betraying sparkle in her eyes, "that I'd hate to be gossiped about by a lot of idle tourists."

"That cool British pride, eh?" He bent his head and his kiss was smoky against her temple. "We start at dawn, *ma fille,* so get a good night's sleep and don't worry about meeting the Emir. He likes pretty women and he will be charming . . . always supposing that he is well enough to meet you."

Kasim rose to his feet with a sigh. "Goodnight, *chérie.*"

"Goodnight, Prince Kasim."

The bead curtain rattled and he was gone. The room seemed empty, but her heart was full. Tears brimmed in her eyes. A sweeter prince was Kasim than many people might suspect.

CHAPTER TWELVE

THE square white residence overlooking Sidi Kebir gave no outward sign of a hidden sumptuousness. A great arched door swept open and they entered an immense courtyard set round with palm trees and fronting the two wings of the palace.

It was in front of the left-hand wing that they dismounted from their tired horses, who were at once led away to the stables while the Shaikh ushered Lorna up a flight of steps and in through another arched door. His retinue of men went in another direction. This part, Lorna guessed, was private to the son of the Emir.

As soon as they entered the reception hall, servants appeared with cool drinks. Kasim spoke to them in crisp Arabic and they went hurrying away to attend to his orders. Then, lighting a cigaret, he turned his attention to Lorna, who had sat down on a divan and was gazing around the hall with wide eyes.

The rich strangeness of her surroundings made her feel tongue-tied. There were cloistered archways and a fountain in the center of the hall set with blue tiles. Cedarwood screens carved into lace-like patterns, tinted hanging lamps, a mosaic floor and walls covered with silken tapestries. Over all hung the scent of sandalwood and a delightful hush.

"It's like the Arabian Nights," Lorna murmured, and it flooded over her that she was in his father's palace and that her position was a rather invidious one.

"You feel strange?" He glanced around him. "I am inclined to feel that way myself when I come from the encampment and find myself beneath a roof once more. I miss the blue sky over the wide free desert.

Lorna raised her eyes to his face in a rather uncertain way. She felt such a stranger, and was even unsure of the man who had brought her here. He looked stern, distant, a slight savagery to his pacing in front of her.

"I must go and see my father," he said. "I will leave you in the hands of Kasha, whom one of the servants will fetch to you. Kasha is the keeper of my apartments, the *kiaya* as we say in Arabic. She was, by the way, my mother's personal maid."

This piece of information made Lorna feel a little easier. She even managed a slight smile as she rose to her feet. "I hope you find your father much improved," she said. "When you do think—" She broke off, biting her lip, for it unnerved her that she must meet the Emir.

"I cannot say." Kasim took her hand and she saw him frown when he found it chilled by nerves. "He won't eat you, *mon enfant*. Like most fathers he likes to take an interest in his son, and having heard rumors about my pearl of the desert—"

"Don't—please!" She wrenched her hand from his just as a woman appeared in the hall. She was tiny and elderly, with a *haik* drawn over her head and halfway across her face. She gave the Prince a bow, and then she looked at Lorna with deep-set eyes that were so dark they seemed to hold many secrets.

"Please take the *lella* to her rooms and see that she has all she needs." He turned and bent to a table to stub his cigaret, and he spoke in French to let Lorna know that she could converse with Kasha without effort. He glanced at the old woman, his eyes keenly anxious. "How does my father seem today?" he asked.

Kasha spread her hands. "The doctors say he has come through the heart attack without too much damage. The rest is with Allah."

"He can speak?" There was a deep note of concern in the deep voice. "He is not too helpless after being so strong?"

"No, he has not lost his powers of speech." A smile glimmered in Kasha's eyes as she surveyed the tall and dominating man she must at one time have dandled on her knee. "He has things to say to his son, who makes the desert his home for months at a time."

"I meant to return earlier." His eyes flicked over Lorna's slim figure. "The desert holds an enchantment I find hard to resist. A man never knows what he will find there."

With a brief bow and a smile, he swung on his heel and strode across the hall to an arched door, which framed him a moment and then was empty. Lorna met the eyes of the old and trusted servant who had been there when Kasim's mother came as a bride. She tried to look composed. "I hope we will

153

be friends, Kasha," she said, forcing herself to smile.

The dark eyes flicked over her riding breeches, and the *shesh* that still covered her hair. There was curiosity in Kasha's glance, but she did not look unkind. "If you will come with me, *lella*, I will show you where you can bathe and relax after your long ride."

They mounted a flight of winding stairs and walked along a fretwork gallery, and plainly across the Eastern rooftops came the wail of a *muezzin* calling the devoted to prayer. It was a sound that made Lorna feel a little melancholy, reminding her that she was no longer in the desert but in the city of Sidi Kebir.

They arrived at the arched doorway of the apartment set aside for Lorna, with a surround of indented leaves and flowers. There was an Arabic inscription in white and gold above the doorway and Lorna paused to study it. "What do the words say?" she asked Kasha.

Kasha gave her a considering look. "Love, say the words, is the gateway to the pomegranate garden. Who plucks the pomegranate shall know sweetness."

Lorna flushed slightly, for it seemed to her that Kasha spoke the words meaningly.

"Will my lady enter the *haremlik?*" the old woman murmured.

There were three rooms, each one separated by a screened doorway of carved wood. In the main room there were divans on raised steps and arabesqued lamps suspended on chains from the painted ceiling. The rugs glowed like jewels upon the floor, and the narrow windows were covered with a lacing of ironwork.

The Arabian furniture in the bedroom was set with mother-of-pearl. Curtains of fine lace were looped about the gilded bed, and on the pearl-inlaid dressing table there was an assortment of cosmetics and several scent bottles.

The bathroom was a joy to behold! It was dominated by a sunken bath of jade green tiles, encircled by a cool arcade in which masses of golden acacia bloomed in huge copper bowls. There were closets ornamented with scrolls, and inside one of them there were enough bath essences and toiletries to serve a dozen girls.

Lorna shut her mind to that thought. This was the *haremlik* of the Sidi Kasim ben Hussayn. It was natural that it would be stocked with scents and silks and oriental slippers.

The great sunken bath was filled from a tap, and Kasha scattered rose essence into the warm, lucent water. Lorna slipped out of her dusty riding clothes and was soon in the bath. She frolicked about in the water, while Kasha looked through a closet and selected wisps of underthings for her new mistress, and a lovely silk robe of jasmine-blue, the border of each hanging sleeve rich with silver embroidery.

Lorna loved the robe from the moment she slipped into it. With her fair shining hair and her deep-blue eyes she looked as lovely as a medieval girl. The silk was so luscious that she couldn't keep from stroking it.

"There is coffee for my lady in the adjoining room," said Kasha, and Lorna found again that the dark eyes were studying her with a curiosity tinged with a certain compassion. It was a look that made Lorna want to ask a certain question. One that had been clamoring in her ever since she had arrived at the palace of the Emir Hussayn.

"Yes, *lella?*" Kasha looked inquiring as Lorna stood hesitant before the arched doorway that led into the other room.

"The Prince Kasim told me that you were his mother's maid." A pink flush came and went in Lorna's cheeks. "What was she like, Kasha? I should love to know."

"My lady Elena was very beautiful."

"I mean . . . what was she like to *know?*" Lorna sat down and poured herself a cup of coffee. "Was she . . . happy?"

A mask of reserve seemed to cover Kasha's face. "She was the Emir's favorite wife, *lella.*"

"He had more than one wife, Kasha?" Lorna gazed stunned over the rim of her coffee cup.

"But of course." Kasha spread her hands in the oriental way and her eyes were faintly amused. "Did you not know that my lord Hussayn had two wives? The sister of the Sidi Kasim was not born to my lady Elena. After the *sidi's* birth she could bear no more children, so the Emir married again. It is the custom. It does not mean that a man loses his love for his first wife."

Lorna sat very still and slim in her blue silk, and it came home forcibly to her that she was among strangers in a far land, whose customs were strange and exotic. Here the men could take more than one wife if they wished . . . here the men did not give their love to one woman alone!

She gave a little shiver beneath the jeweled light of the lamps overhead. She sipped her coffee and tried to find some warmth in it as Kasha quietly withdrew, leaving her alone.

She was not alone for long. Suddenly and silently a girl appeared in the room. She stood between a pair of columns and her darkly fringed eyes were fixed upon Lorna, spice-brown, almond-shaped eyes set in a small, golden-skinned face. Her soft smile showed her flawless teeth. There was a dark beauty spot on her cheekbone, and she wore a silken *melhaffa,* draped perfectly on her slender figure.

"So," she gave a soft, enchanting laugh, "you are the little falcon my brother brings home on his wrist?" She spoke in French with a charming accent. "We had word that your hair was the color of wild honey."

"You are Turqeya!" Lorna stared in her turn at this exotic young creature whose brows were painted to meet across her shapely nose, and whose fingernails were lightly hennaed. A young enchantress!

"Please come and join me," she invited. "The coffee is hot and delicious."

Turqeya came at once and curled down on a sofa facing Lorna. "I am so pleased to meet you," she said. "I was curious about you, but now I can see that you are nice."

Lorna smiled, for her relief at finding Turqeya so friendly went deep. She handed her a cup of coffee and gestured at the mixture of cakes on the low table. "I am happy to meet you, Turqeya," she replied.

"It is true that you rode all over the desert with Kasim on one of his Arab horses? The desert is so vast—did it not frighten you to be in it?"

"I loved the desert." Lorna sipped her second cup of coffee. "I was with your brother, so I wasn't afraid. A few days ago we were together in a sandstorm and it was exhilarating—after the danger was over."

"Men like my brother don't usually make riding companions of women." Turqeya swept her eyes over Lorna, who looked very feminine and even a little fragile in her blue silk robe. "I think you have cast a spell over him. He has always had a fondness for blue jasmine and your eyes are exactly the same color—deep blue with a hint of violet."

"You're kind to say so." Lorna was feeling more relaxed now, in this jewel of a room and in the company of Kasim's delightful young sister.

"Is Kasim kind to you?"

"When he's in the mood." Lorna lashes shaded her eyes as she set down her cup. "How big the palace is! I am longing to explore, especially the gardens which I am sure are full of exotic blooms and wonderful old fountains."

"It has grown too dark for you to see the blue jasmine, but you can smell it. Come!" Turqeya uncurled herself and caught at Lorna's hand. She drew her to the glass doors that led out to a balcony, which was enclosed by a gold-painted grid.

Scent of the jasmine that starred the walls and pergolas below arose on the evening air, delicate and pervasive, and Lorna found herself gripping the iron grid and breathing deeply of the intoxicating scent. Somewhere among the rose and almond trees a bird sang, while overhead a new moon was emerging. Etched by its light were the minarets and domes of Sidi Kebir . . . a silver city, entranced by moonlight.

Lorna's pleasure was a little blue and yearning. It secretly thrilled her that Kasim should think her eyes like his favorite flower, but at the same time she could not help but realize that like the flowers she could not linger here for ever.

"I hope your father recovers soon from his illness," she said to Turqeya.

The girl gave a sigh. "I am sad for him, but I am troubled also for Kasim. He has always been a desert hawk, and now his wings must be clipped. It is feared, you see, that our father will not recover his full powers, and Kasim is the only son, the one who must take the scarlet cloak."

Lorna turned puzzled eyes to the girl.

"The scarlet cloak signifies the chief leader of an Arabian tribe," Turqeya explained. "The people of the beni Saadi adore Kasim because he is handsome, fearless, and virile. He bows down to only the Emir, and even with him he is not afraid to express what is in his heart."

"Is your father very formidable?" Lorna asked nervously.

"Not in the way he used to be. When I was little he used to alarm me when he came to visit my mother. I would run and hide from him in one of my mother's marriage chests. Sometimes when he was in a gentle mood he would come searching for me, and he would pop sweets between my lips. I think it pleased him that I was quite pretty, but he always wanted another son. If there had been a brother for Kasim, he might now be free to lead his own life.

"As it is—" Turqeya shrugged eloquently, and her anklets tinkled as she went back into the room of the divans. Lorna followed, feeling suddenly chilled. She went to the *brasero* to warm her hands.

"Do you like your apartment?" Turqeya asked, and once again she curled down among the big embroidered cushions of the sofa and took a honey tart from the table. She was like a small golden cat, and already Lorna felt fond of her. She was a delectable little half-sister for the splendid, active Kasim who must give up the desert life he loved beyond anything else.

Lorna glanced around at the inlaid furniture, the tiling overlaid by a crusting of arabesques, and the lamps with their jewel colors.

"Did Kasim's mother live here?" she asked, for somehow the atmosphere seemed a little sad despite the splendor, and again she was assailed by the belief that the lady Elena had not been completely happy. As a European woman she must have found the enclosed life—expected then of a Moslem's wife—not entirely to her liking. From what Turqeya had said about her father, he must once have been a very autocratic man.

"Yes, Kasim's mother had this apartment." Turqeya wiped honey from her lips. "My mother was Turkish. It would seem that the men of our family like the women of foreign lands."

Lorna met the brown and teasing eyes, and she said a trifle pensively: "You realize that I am but the guest of your brother?"

Turgeya gazed at Lorna in some perplexity.

"You are so lovely and yet you have been but a companion with whom he has taken rides across the desert? Are British girls less susceptible to the good looks and fascination of a man such as Kasim? Many women in your place would have tried to win his heart."

"I think, Turqeya, that his heart belongs to the desert."

"Is it possible, Lorna, that your heart belongs to Kasim?"

"My cool British reserve was not proof against his charm," Lorna admitted. "At first I thought him a despot, and then I found that he could be strangely kind. Only a few days ago he dared a desert storm in order to look for me when I—ran away from him."

"A woman sometimes runs from what she cannot help loving." Turqeya lowered her long lashes. "Sometimes a man retreats from what he cannot have."

As Lorna pondered the words, Turqeya hid her exotic little face behind her filmy veil, as if she had a secret to hide. Lorna recalled what Zahra had said about the Shaikh, that he had taken it upon himself to choose the man he thought worthy of Turqeya. Suddenly with a tinkling of anklets the pretty girl uncurled from the sofa and ran to throw her arms about the tall figure just entering the room.

He held her and kissed her cheeks and his eyes were warm. "You grow more delectable each time I see you, little one."

"Kasim, you are so brown and fit—so strong that I am afraid you will break me in half!"

"Child, it seems but yesterday that you played

161

hide and seek in the palm groves; now you have *kohl* on your eyes." He shook his head at her. "Cosmetics hide a fresh young skin, and I would advise you to wash off the paint."

She pouted up at him. "You stay so long in the desert that you become old-fashioned, brother. Here in the city a girl likes to look chic."

"Chic?" he teased. "Cleopatra used *kohl* on her eyes and paint on her face." He put his thumb against the beauty spot on Turqeya's cheekbone and carefully erased it. "My little sister, you don't need the tricks of a Nile dancer to make you attractive."

"You are a brute, Kasim!" Turqeya lightly slapped his hard brown cheek. "If I were Lorna I would run away from you!"

He flashed a look at Lorna and his eyes glinted as he took in the blue gown that she wore. The lustrous material matched her eyes and glowed against her fair skin and shining hair.

"How did you find your father?" she asked him.

"He seems to be regaining strength and was able to talk to me about things which have been worrying him."

"He has wanted you to come home—oh, so much, Kasim!" Turqeya ran a hand along her brother's broad shoulder. "You must promise not to go away again."

He was gazing over his sister's head and Lorna alone saw the bleak look that came into his tawny eyes. It distressed her that he should look like that. His longing for the desert was a yearning she could not hope to assuage. The desert was the love of his life . . . she was but an interlude.

162

Turqeya stayed talking to them for about an hour, and then she left them to dine alone. As in their desert tent, their meal was brought to them by Hassan, who had returned to Sidi Kebir with his master.

"Do you like what you have so far seen of the palace?" The Shaikh spoke as he ate, as if with an effort.

"It's like something out of an Arabian fable," she said. "I would treasure so many antique and lovely things if it were my home."

She felt his quick glance, but he continued to eat in silence and she was glad when the meal came to an end.

"Would you like to go to the roof terrace and see the city by moonlight?" He drew her to her feet and it was a subtle torment to be so close to him after an entire day that had held them apart.

"Very much," she said.

He held her and gazed down into her eyes, a rather searching light in his own eyes. "I will fetch you a cloak. Our sunshine is hot, but our moonlight is cold."

He strode into the adjoining room and she awaited his return with a pensive, uncertain air about her. In the desert she had known hell and heaven with him . . . but nothing could touch the subtle torture of being with him in the house of his boyhood. Lorna glanced about her, as if seeking the slender woman who seemed to haunt these rooms . . . watching as Kasim came to her and fastened about her sholders a cloak of thick glossy silk, its silvery sheen that of the moonlight he wished to share with her.

They left the apartment through a sculptured doorway and went along the fretted gallery to a stairway, narrow and winding, and leading to the rooftop that overlooked the shadow and mystery of Sidi Kebir.

The luminous light of the new moon seemed to intensify the stillness of the night. Far below lay the walled gardens and narrow streets, wending their way into the heart of the city. Strange vibrations could be felt, spicy aromas hung on the air, and wicked deeds of the past could still be felt in this timeless land. The drifting sound of Arabian music added to the enchantment.

"It's like a black and silver tapestry," Lorna murmured, and the scents of the night, the air of the forbidden, sapped from her the will to move away from the Shaikh. She felt him beside her, so tall and lithe in his *kaftan* and narrow trousers. Her heart beat fast, his slightest touch thrilled through her like tiny, exquisitely painful arrows.

"The moonlight is in your hair," he said quietly. "You are part of the mystery and the tapestry."

As his breath stirred her hair, she wanted in a panic of love to run from him, and at the same time she wanted to lay her head against his shoulder and ask him to love her in return.

If only he loved her, how wonderful the night, how fearless the future.

"Tomorrow I take you to see the Emir." His hand touched her shoulder. "He has expressed a wish to see you."

A little shiver of apprehension ran through her. What if the Emir objected to her presence at the palace? What if he told Kasim to send her away?

Kasha had hinted that he was a man of absolute authority, and Turqeya spoke of him with admiration rather than the affection of a daughter.

Lorna gazed down upon the moonlit city and thought of her own love for her own dear father. How he would have enjoyed painting a city such as Sidi Kebir, its domes and minarets would have pleased his artistic eye so much.

She looked at Kasim and saw how stern his face was in the moonlight. It was obvious that he had something on his mind, something he wouldn't tell her.

"Perhaps it would have been better if I had chosen to go to Yraa," she said. "I don't wish to complicate life for you, Kasim. Not with your father lying ill."

"You have a gentle heart, Lorna." His arms stole round her and held her against the indented wall. "And I could not be as heartless as to set you free without making amends for stealing you."

"Amends?" she whispered, and she couldn't tell if it was her heart or his that beat so furiously. Even the moonlight could not have come between them as he held her by the parapet and the night wind blew her hair into a soft cloud.

"Tomorrow," his eyes held hers, "You will know, *petite.*"

CHAPTER THIRTEEN

LORNA ran quietly down the stairs that led to the gardens of the palace. It was very early and she had a need to be alone for a while.

An arched doorway framed her slim figure, and then she was out under an arcade and facing a rose garden damp with dew. She took a deep breath of the fresh, scented air and very soon had lost herself among the trees with their deep red flowers piled high and festooning downward in fragrant clusters.

She wandered beneath tunnels of blue jasmine and into the groves of palm and cypress. She glimpsed a sunbird, whose plumage was a dazzling mixture of blue and green. When she came to a small walled patio she paused to admire a fountain in which the water tumbled from basin to basin, creating a waterfall effect. She sat down on a tiled bench and was so still, so entranced, that birds came unafraid to drink at the fountain and to flap their feathers in the water.

A transient peace stole over Lorna, though her pulses fluttered in time with the butterflies each time she thought of the morning ahead of her, and the meeting Kasim had arranged between her and his formidable father.

Her gaze dwelt on the oleander bushes, whose glossy leaves harbored a poisonous sap. Sun and shadow made arabesques . . . even here the bitter mingled with the sweetness of petal and scent.

A sigh escaped her. How nice to be a bird who could take wing and fly away and leave no shadow, only a memory of having lingered awhile.

She could not fathom what Kasim had meant when he talked last night of making amends today. After they had left the roof terrace he had gone to wish his father a good night, and he had not returned to her.

A butterfly hovered on the petals of a sunflower close by. It was golden, like the flash of gold through the dark lashes of Kasim's eyes. Her heart quivered like the wings of the butterfly. Her heart clutched for a reason why she should love a man who had made her his toy.

She would never betray herself by telling him of her own feelings. If the time had come for them to part . . . she crushed a rose she had plucked and her pain was made physical as a thorn sharply pierced her. She sucked the tiny wound. If only her parting from the Shaikh could be so swift a pain.

As the sun arose and shone through the palm trees, she left the peaceful little patio and wandered back beneath the tunnels of jasmine, burning blue in the sunlight, and saw cowled figures working among the trees of the groves. The air had grown honey-warm and the sun was opening the roses. The petals were soundless as they fell . . . a rose died as a memory died, in silence and without visible pain. The heart held its pain as the thorny bush held the last of the rose.

167

As she reached the cool arcade that led into the palace, a snowy Persian kitten detached itself from the shadows and came to wind itself about Lorna's ankles. She knelt on the warmth of the tiles to play with it, charmed by its emerald green eyes and its purring friendliness. "You darling!" Lorna laughed her delight as the kitten rolled over and nuzzled her fingers with its tiny damp nose.

She was absorbed in her play with the kitten when footsteps paused on the tiles of the arcade. She glanced up and found Kasim watching her. He stood very still, etched in sunlight and shadow. He wore a dark *burnous* embroidered with gold, and leather knee-boots moulded to his feet and legs. His eyes were very still, and they held an expression she had never seen in them before . . . one of pain.

"What is the matter?" She scrambled to her feet and the kitten darted away in alarm. "Is your father not so well today?"

"Yes . . . he makes progress." In a couple of strides Kasim came to her and took hold of her hands. He studied them, and then he looked into her eyes.

"You looked but a child playing with that kitten," he said.

She didn't feel like a child . . . no woman ever could with Kasim. He was too much a man, so tall and somehow stern in the immaculate robes that suited him so well. *Shaikh el Arabe.* She loved him for all the reasons that in the beginning had made her afraid of him.

"We are to go to the Emir in one hour." He pressed her hands encouragingly. "Tell Kasha that you are to be dressed in something very charming."

"I am nervous," she admitted. "What will he think of me?"

"My dear," his smile was whimsical, "an Arabian such as the Emir does not look beyond the face of a woman. He will think you quite lovely."

Then he lifted her hands and kissed them briefly. "Go to Kasha," he smiled.

Lorna gazed after him as he strode toward another section of the palace. The folds of his *burnous* were sculptured around his figure. There was an air of gravity about him that perplexed her . . . it intensified her feeling that this meeting with his father was a prelude to her departure.

When she reached her apartment she found Kasha waiting to help her dress, but first she took a cool dip in the sunken bath and emerged feeling fresh and ready for her encounter with the Emir.

Kasha brushed her hair until it shone, and then she was attired in a long silk dress overlaid by a diaphanous tunic with embroidered sleeves that fell away at the bend of the elbow. A little jewelled cap was placed upon her head and the veiling was pinned by a jewel to the shoulder of her dress. She slipped her feet into pearl-colored shoes, and when she turned to face her reflection in the painted mirror, she caught her breath.

"The *lella* is indeed the pearl of the Sidi Kasim." Kasha straightened the yards of veiling and smiled with satisfaction. "Within his blood his mother's love of beauty, within his very bones his devil of a father, it is no wonder that he took you for his own."

Lorna caught her breath. "I am to meet his father and I am very nervous, Kasha."

The old lady stared into Lorna's eyes in the mirror, and then with a smile she touched a strand of Lorna's fair hair. "The Emir is not the stern man he was before his illness. You need not fear him."

But Lorna feared his power. She was quite certain that he was going to tell her that she must part from his son.

Kasim came for her, and she wore over the silk dress the cloak in which she had shared last night's moonlight with him. They traversed the long corridors of the palace, decorated with the many curved and gilded archways of an Arabian dwelling. At last they came to a massive door in which a golden crescent was set.

They entered a reception room of much grandeur, in which a Sultan of old might have lounged on a divan to drink sherbet and listen to music with a favorite *kadin* beside him.

Lorna glanced at Kasim and her blue eyes were large with questions. He looked very princely, quickening her heart in his black and gold, his headcloth encircled by the gold ropes of his important position. His attire, combined with his upright bearing and his look of sternness, made her feel a stranger to him.

"Please tell me!" The words could be held in no longer. "I know I am to be sent away!"

His eyes dwelt on her and there was a flare to his nostrils, as if he rebelled against the idea of losing her. As if he still wanted her companionship as much as he had in the desert. He opened his lips as if to speak, but in that moment a white-clad servant appeared and they were asked politely to please follow him.

170

A moment more and they were in the presence of the Emir Hussayn ben Mansour beni Saadi, head of the great Arabian clan who traced their beginnings beyond the Crusades.

He had great blazing eyes and the hard features of a ruler. A proud old *pasha* with pillows banked behind his head as he lay in a bed with an immense canopy that reached to the ceiling.

He gazed for a long moment at Lorna, who looked lost and lovely in her Arabian finery. His gaze dwelt on the veil she clutched with her fingers but did not hide behind. Then he looked slowly at Kasim, who stood tall, dark, and silent at the foot of the great bed. There were other people in the room who stood equally silent, officials in flowing robes.

"So, my son," the Emir began slowly to smile and at once there seemed a lessening of tension in the room. "So this is the fair *roumia* you would take as a wife, eh?"

There was it seemed to Lorna a clap of thunder, and then an intense silence. She glanced dazedly at Kasim. It couldn't be true! She must be having a dream . . . a wildly impossible dream!

Then she saw a faintly sardonic smile curve on his lips as he caught her look. "My father wishes me to take a wife and I have chosen to take you," he said deliberately.

She stood speechless, and was aware that everyone in the room was looking at her. The Shaikh had spoken last night of making amends and this was it! The *amende honorable* and nothing less!

A ceiling fan purred hypnotically, and now she

171

knew why she was dressed in silk and veiling . . . the marriage was to take place here, the vows were to be spoken over the imperial bed of the Emir!

Lorna wanted to protest, to cry out *no*, not like this, without love or tenderness or any hope of a lasting happiness! There could be no joy or happiness without Kasim's love. It was the giving of his heart that she longed for.

But even as protest clamored in her, she recalled unforgettable moments with him. Their rides across the desert sands beneath the dawn sky . . . sharing the danger of the sandstorm with him and being taken for a boy by the friendly nomads.

The power and mystery of him held her in thrall. If this was what he wanted, then she could not fight his will.

She bowed her head to let all of them know that she was willing to become his bride. In a daze she heard the Arabic words spoken by a robed official, and she touched the exquisite lettering of the Koran. Her eyes were dazzled by the jeweled scimitar which was poised over her head, symbol of the authority of her Arabian husband. Yes, just a few words and he became her husband!

After the brief ceremony the Emir beckoned to her and she went to the bedside. The bed was so high that she was on a level with him as he dropped over her head a shimmering necklace. "You are now of the beni Saadi, my daughter. It is a grave moment, eh?" He smiled, but she saw the weariness in his face that was like a mask of bronze battered by the years. He took her hands into his and she felt their frailty. It was for the Emir's sake that Kasim had married her!

"This marriage has my blessing," he said tiredly, "and I hope that it will be many times blessed for the beni Saadi."

"Thank you, my lord," she murmured, and then she was ushered into the adjoining room and was swathed in a sumptuous cloak and carried in a litter from the father's section of the palace to that of the son's.

The news of the marriage was speedily announced from minarets all over the city. Lorna, resting alone in her apartment, heard the cries of *Allah akbar,* and soon afterward there was a round of fireworks as the people flocked into the streets to celebrate the marriage.

She was still in a dream state and couldn't fully arouse from it even when Turqeya came to tell her that a party of women had arrived to give their good wishes to the bride. Lorna could hear them laughing and chattering in the adjoining room, and she shrank from going among them and putting on the mask of a happy bride.

"What is it, my sister?" Turqeya's smile died away as she caught the look of quiet despair in Lorna's eyes. "I thought you loved Kasim! To marry him was surely your greatest desire?"

"To marry him knowing I had his love." Lorna played restlessly with his star-sapphire ring. "You are a woman, Turqeya. You must know how I feel."

"Yes." Turqeya's eyes brooded on the sapphire that burned blue like Lorna's eyes. "As an Arabian girl I live with the fear that I will be made to marry against my will. How could I marry anyone else where for years, since I was a child of twelve, I have

173

had a place in my heart for only one man. He is not a prince, nor is he rich, but I love him with all my heart."

Turqeya sat down beside Lorna and caught at her hands. "I had the hope that now you are my sister and Kasim's wife, you would intercede for me and tell him that I cannot marry at all if I cannot be allowed to marry Omair. . . ."

"Omair ben Zaide?" The blue eyes clung to the brown ones, and suddenly there were tears on Turqeya's lashes.

"You have spoken with him?" she asked eagerly. "You like him?"

"Very much indeed." Lorna wiped a tear from Turqeya's cheek. "He is a fine person, Turqeya, so why should Kasim object to a marriage between you?"

"Omair has only his doctor's pay, and he fears that if he asked for my hand, my brother would refuse permission on the grounds that I am the only daughter of the Emir of Sidi Kebir."

"But," Lorna smiled perplexedly, "Kasim has married *me* and he is the only son of the Emir."

"It is different." Turqeya spoke with downcast eyes. "Your children will be Kasim's and he is a prince of the beni Saadi. If I were permitted to marry Omair then our children would not have titles and distinction."

"They would have love," Lorna said warmly. "Turqeya, I am sure you are both wrong in your judgment of Kasim. Omair is his friend. I am sure he would be delighted to have him for a brother. I am even more certain that he doesn't wish to force you into a loveless marriage."

174

"He has forced you to marry him! You have said, Lorna, that you don't possess his heart."

It was an unbearable truth, one from which Lorna dragged her thoughts. "You must be made happy, Turqeya," she said firmly. "I shall speak to Kasim and I promise you—"

She never finished the sentence, for Turqeya flung joyful arms around her and hugged her until she was breathless. "I knew from the moment we met that you had a generous heart! I knew I could be friends with you, and it gives me great joy that we are now sisters!"

Lorna kissed the soft young cheek—fresh and unpainted—and felt the brush of her hoop earring studded with small jewels. She breathed the Eastern perfume that the girl wore, and it rushed over her that she had married into an Arabian family and would have to abide by the rules that dominated the wife of a prince.

Lorna forced a smile to her lips. "Let us go into the other room." She jumped to her feet. "We are keeping our guests waiting."

The women were delighted with her. They fingered her hair and her person with a beguiling curiosity, and informed her that she was like a flower.

A zither and drums were played, and the company sat on the divans and drank coffee and ate rich pastries and sweets. They were clad in embroidered dresses and their arms and ankles tinkled with jewellery. Their speaking hands were painted with henna, and their perfume was dizzying.

Lorna sat among them, the target of all their

175

chatter and their quips, but she didn't understand very much of what they said. Later a great dish of *cous-cous* was brought in, stuffed with roast lamb, legs of chicken, ortolans, and apricots.

Being the bride she was not allowed to exert herself, and the laughing women fed her like a cuckoo by popping piquant morsels of food between her lips. At any other time she would have been very amused, but her thoughts were constantly with Kasim, who was among the male guests down in the courtyard of the palace.

It was close on midnight when Lorna, the bride, was lighted into the bedroom by candles held aloft by the women guests. Charms were strewn about to avert the evil eye, and dates and milk were placed beside the nuptial bed. Old Kasha came to help her undress, for she must be entirely unadorned for her bridegroom.

"The *lella* looks a little pale," Kasha murmured. "A wedding day is a trying day, and I am reminded of my lady Elena and how nervous she was on her wedding night."

Lorna gave a shiver, and her gaze dwelt on the silken shift that lay like a handful of mist on the embroidered cover of the bed.

"Was the lady Elena happy in her marriage?" she asked at last.

Kasha did not reply for several moments, and then she said quietly. "My lady adjusted in time to the life . . . and there were compensations."

"You mean the birth of her son, Kasim?"

"Yes, *lella,* I mean the birth of the Sidi Kasim."

"He must have been a fine child." Lorna's hands

176

clenched the transparent shift. "I expect his mother spoiled him?"

"The lady Elena took a great delight in her baby boy . . . my lord the Emir took an even greater pride in him."

"Kasim was the only son?"

"Yes, *lella,* the only boy the Emir was to have for his heir."

Left alone at last, Lorna wandered restlessly about the lamplit bedroom. Beyond the closed door the sounds of merriment continued . . . and then quite suddenly all went quiet and Lorna's loudly beating heart told her that her husband was about to come to her.

Clad in the gossamer robe she backed away from the door to the edge of the bed. She felt as trapped tonight as in his tent in the desert . . . if only he came to her with a fiery love in his heart!

The door swept open and he stood framed there a moment before closing it firmly behind him. He wore a rich *kaftan* of saffron silk swinging back from the creamy silk of his tunic. The sleeves of the *kaftan* were bordered with gold thread, and a golden cord bound his snowy turban. His feet were encased in yellow slippers, and he looked as splendid as a prince of the Arabian Nights.

Lorna stared at him with great blue eyes. Love and fear raged in her like a flame . . . he was now her husband and never before had she felt so completely in his power.

His eyes wandered over her . . . and it was then that the unnerving events of the day took their toll of her and every bit of strength ebbed out of her. She swayed where she stood and would have fallen if Kasim had not taken a quick stride forward and caught her in his arms. He lifted her and laid her on the bed. He leaned over her and stroked her pale cheeks.

"Poor *petite,*" he murmured. "It has all been a little too much for you, eh?

She lay beneath the spread of his shoulders, snared by love, by this marriage which was made to please a man who might be dying. "So this was what you meant last night," she said huskily. "The *amende honorable.* A marriage made to content the Emir."

"In part, Lorna," he admitted, and there fell a little silence that seemed to tremble between them. "If we had discussed it when alone last night, you might have found it impossible to agree to the idea let alone the actuality. Also there was the shadow to erase, which I had cast upon your honor. Now you share with me a much honored name in this part of the world."

She gazed up at him, taking in each detail of his darkly handsome face in the amber lamplight. A beloved face, a heart-shaking closeness of body . . . a distance of heart that only a mutual love could ever bridge. "I have heard that it takes only a few words for an Arabian to discard a wife . . . if he doesn't love her."

"Shall I speak them, Lorna, and let you return to your own world?"

"My world?" Her smile was bittersweet. "You gave me the desert and showed me the way to the stars. You gave me the dawn, and now you would send me out into the darkness."

"You grew to love so much the desert that we

shared?" His arm cradled her, his eyes smoldered. "What happened to the rebellion in your heart? Why, only a few days ago you tried to run away from me . . . from the dawns we shared, from the desert stars. But for the storm you might have got away . . . now you dare me to believe that you really wish to stay with me. Lorna, *ma fille,* do you wish to stay married to me?"

She gazed back at him with a deep shyness in her eyes. *"M'sieu,* you have me at a disadvantage."

"Meaning you are too shy to ask me if I wish to remain married to you?"

"I should like you to wish it for your own sake," she found the courage to say, and as she suffered his tawny gaze upon her, and felt the wonderful strength of him, she tossed from her the few rags of pride that meant nothing any more. "I am yours to keep, if you wish, Kasim. Yours to discard."

"Mine?" Suddenly his arms crushed her to him, so that he hurt her in the most joyful way. *"Mon amour adoré. Mon ange,* so sweet, so gallant, so full of goodness that you shame the devil in my heart. My love, my eyes, my very life. I knew it from the moment I saw you and I had to carry you off, or lose you for ever. I had to show you my desert and woo you with rides *l'aube,* with passionate sunsets, and silver moonlight. You were part of all these with your own silver-fair beauty . . . !"

He broke off and buried his face in her hair. "I longed for you to care, and to forgive my arrogance. Do you care . . . do you forgive me for riding off with you? You were like a dream I could not let go of . . . do you understand?"

"Oh . . . Kasim." Her hands pressed close

against the strong neck that carried his proud head. Never before had he bent that head to anyone, now he bent it to her. "I realized that I loved you while the sandstorm raged. You talked of us dying together, of being choked for all time in each other's arms. I would want to die if I couldn't be with you."

She spoke his name again and he took his name from her lips, a kiss so piercingly sweet that she could have died. "Our marriage must be a real one, Lorna. Abiding and honest, with no secrets ever between us."

"Have you secrets, Kasim?" She laughed softly, for it seemed in the sweetness of this moment that nothing mattered except that he loved her and held her in his arms. She felt weak in his strong arms, no longer the little icicle who had scoffed at love in the garden of the Ras Jusuf. A real desert man had melted her. . . .

"Yes, there is something I must tell you, *cherie*." He kissed her eyes, and then he reached for a cigaret from the box on the bedside table. She lay and watched him as he lit it, and her heart quickened. What was he about to tell her? That he had loved someone else before *le destin* had brought them together? She told herself that she would be indulgent, but all the time she hoped that he had never loved anyone but her.

He smoked in silence for a few minutes, as if to get his thoughts into order, and for the first time she noticed the mass of blue jasmine in a pewter vase. Its scent mingled with the smoke of his cigaret, and suddenly on a low carved bureau she saw in a silver frame the portrait of a boy. His hair was dark and tousled, his eyes were full of the devil, and there was something about him that reminded her of children she had seen playing on the boulevards of Paris.

Kasim saw her studying the picture and he smiled into her eyes. "I was about ten years old when *maman* had that photograph taken of me."

"I should have loved to know you as a boy," she said shyly.

"Far better to know me as a man, *chérie*." His smile was the faintly wicked smile of their desert days. "I hope *maman* knows that I have found myself a girl so lovely and spirited."

"Is there not an Arabian word for mother?" she asked, intrigued.

"There is, of course, but I never used it. My mother wished me to call her *maman* from the moment I could speak."

"Why was that, Kasim?" Lorna looked at him with the tender eyes of a girl beloved. "Did she ever tell you why?"

"I think she meant to," his eyes were thoughtful through the smoke that twined about his lean, suntanned face. His eyes dwelt on Lorna, fair and young in the big Arabian bed, her eyes the color of the blue jasmine scenting the bedroom, her lips love-kissed.

Suddenly Kasim reached for her hand and took it to his lips and kissed each finger in the Gallic way. "It was also my mother's wish that I learn Spanish as well as French. She kept a diary that after her death no one could read but me. There were pages that I tore out and destroyed after I had read them . . . they revealed the secret she could share

181

only with me. Now I intend to share it with you, Lorna, because you love me, because you have said that you wish to stay with me as my wife."

Lorna gazed at him with wondering eyes. "I thought you meant to tell me you had loved someone else before we met."

"Girls?" He quirked an eyebrow. "A few in Paris during the years I was a student. I shared a little laughter and gaiety with them, but my heart was never involved. I loved the desert . . . she was the woman for me . . . until you came into my life, blue-eyed, with sunshine-colored hair and all the temperament of the desert."

"Did no lovely Arabian girl ever take your eye, Kasim?" she asked teasingly.

His answering smile was a little strange. "Some of them are very lovely, like Turqeya, but it would seem that my instincts were always French and that. . . ."

"French?" Lorna exclaimed.

"Yes." His fingers gripped hers. "I am not the son of the Emir, but the son of a Frenchman who came to Sidi Kebir a year after my mother came here as a bride."

In the silence that followed his thunderbolt, Lorna could have counted her heartbeats. Her eyes were fixed upon Kasim, a blue and eager light in them. Outside in the palace gardens a nightingale was singing, and it was as if her heart broke into song.

"Please," she whispered, "please tell me everything."

Kasim bowed his head slightly, as if never before he had talked of things his mother had revealed in her Spanish diary. As if, even with Lorna, he found it a little hard to speak of a secret that was rather painful.

"He came, this man, from *la belle* France. My mother was not too happy with her life, which she found enclosed, strange to her, and this Frenchman was a diversion for her. He was young but learned, and he came to investigate some scrolls found in an old vault of the palace. He was charming, very much of the world my mother had left when she married the Emir. Soon she was admitting in her diary to a guilty happiness in the company of Justin."

Kasim glanced up and looked significantly into Lorna's wide, blue, listening eyes. "The Emir was always busy attending to his duties, and when he found time to be with his young wife he treated her as a toy, to be fondled but not made a real companion of. This fellow Justin was not like that. He discussed his work with her. He told her about the countries he had visited. It was inevitable that their friendship turn into a stolen affair of love."

Kasim sighed a little and fondled the star sapphire on Lorna's hand. "The little ostrich played with fire. She dared to be with this man here in this very apartment. She was lonely, and he was fascinating, but their hours of love were numbered of course, and in time his work was completed and he went away. My mother settled down to try and forget him, but soon she knew there was to be a child, and that child would be Justin's not her husband's!

Lorna's husband paused in his narrative, and she could almost feel again—here in this room—

the anguish that his mother must have felt when she realized that her affair with the Frenchman was to bear fruit. Lovely, her long dark hair to her waist, she would have paced about this very room, not regretting the love she had felt for Justin, but afraid for her coming child—his child.

"She must have gone in dread fear for some time," Kasim went on, a deep, moved note in his voice. "But the Emir was desperately eager for a child and as mercy would have it he never suspected that his Elena had been unfaithful to him. I was born and he accepted me without question as his son. Kasha tells me that I was a large, bawling, black-haired infant, and that when I was placed in the Emir's arms he carried me to the forecourt of the palace and showed me proudly to his people as the next heir.

"It was strange, Lorna, but the Arabians always liked me and I had an affinity with them. I loved the hot sun, as they did. Fleet horses, and riding with the wind across the desert. I know my mother always meant to tell me the truth about my birth, but she died suddenly when I was thirteen and I alone could read her diary when it was found among her belongings."

The tawny eyes held Lorna's. "The Emir is sick, perhaps dying, and it is too late to tell him the truth. I must continue to give him loyalty and affection. He needs me, looks to me to carry on with his work, and the bond between us cannot be broken by a secret as old as I am. I think Kasha has always suspected the truth, but she loved my mother too much to ever betray her. Lorna . . .?"

She didn't speak. She leaned forward and

kissed him on the lips, sealing them and their secret. "I love you, Kasim. Whither thou goest, my dear. Whither thou dwellest."

Again his arms held her and crushed her close to his heart. He looked at her and it was as if a flame glowed in his eyes. "The people here in Sidi Kebir are saying that you are like a pearl, Lorna. How right they are, *chérie*. My pearl of the desert. As if I called you to me. Do you think it was my voice you heard?"

"My heart heard it, Kasim." She nestled against his shoulder and breathed the tobacco smoke that always reminded her of her father. "Do you remember the white flower that I carried in my pocket? It made you angry because I said it came from a man I loved. That man was my father. He lived in a house at the Oasis of Fadna and after he died I went to look at the house. It had slowly crumbled away and all that was left was a wall and on that wall some white flowers were still blooming. I plucked one, Kasim. It was all I had to cling to, that first night in your tent. I was so afraid of you. . . ."

"Mon ange," he buried his lips in her hair. "Never be afraid of me ever again!"

"I shall always be a little afraid of you," she laughed softly against his warm throat. "You can look so fierce at times, my desert lover."

He gazed down at her, straight into her eyes, and then he smiled slowly at their unwavering blueness. "I think sometimes we will fight," he murmured. "But afterward we will always kiss."

Lorna smiled and drew his dark head down to her. The nightingale sang in the garden where the blue jasmine starred the moonlit walls and Lorna no longer fled from the arms of her desert lover. Never would either of them be lonely again. They had searched and found the golden garden . . . and it was the garden of love.

Now available!

COLLECTION EDITIONS

of Classic Romances

Harlequin proudly presents a nostalgic collection
of the best-selling romance novels of former years.
This is a rare series of 100 books, lovingly reissued
in beautifully designed new covers. And the cost is
only 75¢ each. See complete listing on
accompanying pages.

Not sold in stores.

Harlequin Collection Editions

2 (#412) **Nurse Trenton**
Caroline Trench

3 (#416) **Doctor Lucy**
Barbara Allen

4 (#423) **City Nurse**
Jane Arbor

5 (#430) **Ship's Nurse**
Alex Stuart

6 (#434) **Dear Doctor
Everett**
Jean S. MacLeod

7 (#500) **Unsteady Flame**
Marjorie Moore

8 (#512) **Australian
Hospital**
Joyce Dingwell

9 (#513) **Far Sanctuary**
Jane Arbor

10 (#517) **Journey
in the Sun**
Jean S. MacLeod

11 (#528) **Wife by
Arrangement**
Mary Burchell

12 (#600) **Jan Marlowe,
Hospital Librarian**
Margaret Malcolm

13 (#601) **Love without
Ending**
Lilian Chisholm

14 (#604) **Flight to the
Stars**
Pamela Kent

15 (#608) **White-Coated
Girl**
Anne Lorraine

16 (#609) **Copper Beeches**
Marjorie Moore

17 (#730) **The Stars of
San Cecilio**
Susan Barrie

18 (#711) **My Heart's in
the Highlands**
Jean S. MacLeod

19 (#712) **House of
Conflict**
Mary Burchell

20 (#704) **Private Case**
Marguerite Lees

21 (#737) **Maiden Flight**
Betty Beaty

22 (#800) **Sweet Waters**
Rosalind Brett

23 (#805) **Love this Enemy**
Kathryn Blair

24 (#835) **Part-Time Angel**
Elizabeth Houghton

25 (#842) **When Love
Is Secret**
Margaret Baumann

26 (#818) **The Second Year**
Valerie K. Nelson

*Please note: The number in brackets indicates the
original Harlequin Romance number.*

Harlequin Collection Editions

27 (#436) **Garrison Hospital**
Alex Stuart

28 (#443) **Nurse on Call**
Elizabeth Gilzean

29 (#449) **Come Back, My Dream**
Elizabeth Hoy

30 (#463) **The Morning Star**
Kate Norway

31 (#492) **Follow a Dream**
Marjorie Moore

32 (#557) **The Time Is Short**
Nerina Hilliard

33 (#564) **Doctor to the Isles**
Juliet Shore

34 (#585) **Nurse to the Cruise**
Anne Vinton

35 (#591) **Hotel Nurse**
Anne Lorraine

36 (#597) **This Much to Give**
Jean S. MacLeod

37 (#610) **Doctor at Hilltops**
Lilian Chisholm

38 (#619) **Staff Nurse on Gynae**
Hilda Pressley

39 (#641) **There Goes My Heart**
Margaret Baumann

40 (#665) **A Problem for Doctor Brett**
Marjorie Norrell

41 (#673) **Gateway to Happiness**
Ann Cameron

42 (#738) **Send for Doctor**
Anne Lorraine

43 (#741) **Journey into Yesterday**
Marjorie Ellison

44 (#752) **The Ordeal of Nurse Thompson**
Nora Sanderson

45 (#775) **That Nice Nurse Nevin**
Jan Tempest

46 (#795) **Back Room Girl**
Marguerite Lees

47 (#802) **South to Forget**
Essie Summers

48 (#851) **A Song for Tomorrow**
Lillian Chisholm

49 (#867) **Elusive Lady**
Anne Lorraine

50 (#868) **This Starry Stranger**
Peta Cameron

51 (#879) **Sweet to Remember**
Anne Weale

*Please note: The number in brackets indicates the
original Harlequin Romance number.*

Harlequin Collection Editions

52 (#433) **Because of Doctor Danville**
Elizabeth Hoy

53 (#439) **Hospital in Sudan**
Anne Vinton

54 (#477) **Hospital Blue**
Anne Vinton

55 (#481) **Bachelor in Medicine**
Alex Stuart

56 (#490) **Nurse MacLean Goes West**
Elizabeth Gilzean

57 (#505) **Meet Dr. Kettering**
Marguerite Lees

58 (#508) **Senior Surgeon**
Marjorie Moore

59 (#518) **Hospital in Paradise**
Juliet Shore

60 (#519) **Doctor Pamela**
Anne Vinton

61 (#529) **Theatre Nurse**
Hilda Pressley

62 (#612) **Patient for Doctor Gaird**
Anne Lorraine

63 (#618) **Doctor Di at the Crossroads**
Anne Vinton

64 (#627) **With All My Worldly Goods**
Mary Burchell

65 (#632) **Love in the Sunlight**
Averil Ives

66 (#634) **Love without Wings**
Margaret Malcolm

67 (#708) **Calling Nurse Grant**
Lilian Chisholm

68 (#713) **Harvest of the Heart**
Jill Christian

69 (#715) **The Heart of a Hospital**
Anne Vinton

70 (#767) **The Silver Dolphin**
Anne Weale

71 (#779) **Mistress of Brown Furrows**
Susan Barrie

72 (#804) **Bladon's Rock**
Pamela Kent

73 (#811) **The Way to the Wedding**
Joan Blair

74 (#831) **Hotel at Treloan**
Susan Barrie

75 (#838) **Dear Dragon**
Sara Seale

76 (#888) **Heart of a Rose**
Rachel Lindsay

Please note: The number in brackets indicates the original Harlequin Romance number.

Harlequin Collection Editions

77 (#459) **Second Love**
Marjorie Moore

78 (#462) **Love from a Surgeon**
Elizabeth Gilzean

79 (#467) **Nurse to the Island**
Caroline Trench

80 (#472) **Young Doctor Kirkdene**
Elizabeth Hoy

81 (#476) **Nurse Jess**
Joyce Dingwell

82 (#509) **A Year to Remember**
Marjorie Moore

83 (#510) **Doctor Halcott**
Marguerite Lees

84 (#530) **Dr. Daring's Love Affair**
Anne Vinton

85 (#535) **Under the Red Cross**
Juliet Shore

86 (#539) **Hospital on Wheels**
Anne Lorraine

87 (#623) **Thursday Clinic**
Anne Lorraine

88 (#636) **Home at Hawk's Nest**
Caroline Trench

89 (#639) **Nurse in Spain**
Alex Stuart

90 (#642) **The White Jacket**
Kate Norway

91 (#648) **Gray's Hospital**
Joan Blair

92 (#720) **General Hospital**
Marguerite Lees

93 (#723) **Fortune Goes Begging**
Margaret Malcolm

94 (#739) **When the Heart Is Young**
Lilian Chisholm

95 (#754) **The Rancher Needs a Wife**
Celine Conway

96 (#757) **The Palm-Thatched Hospital**
Juliet Shore

97 (#815) **Young Tracy**
Rosalind Brett

98 (#836) **He Whom I Love**
Hilda Nickson

99 (#843) **A Summer at Barbazon**
Kathryn Blair

100 (#847) **The Smoke and the Fire**
Essie Summers

101 (#852) **The Fair Stranger**
Valerie K. Nelson

Please note: The number in brackets indicates the original Harlequin Romance number.

Complete and mail this coupon today!